A Finely Tuned
Apathy Machine

A Finely Tuned Apathy Machine

MARK PATERSON

Exile Editions

Publishers of singular
Fiction, Poetry, Drama, Non-fiction and Graphic Books

2007

Library and Archives Canada Cataloguing in Publication

Paterson, Mark, 1971-
    A finely tuned apathy machine / Mark Paterson.

Short stories.

ISBN 978-1-55096-087-7

    I. Title.

PS8631.A832F46 2007   C813'.6   C2007-904591-X

Design and Composition by Homunculus ReproSet
Cover "Mirage" by Susana Wald and Ludwig Zeller
Typeset in Garamond, Birka and Carlton at the Moons of Jupiter Studios
Printed in Canada by Gauvin Imprimerie

The publisher would like to acknowledge the financial assistance of
The Canada Council for the Arts, and the Ontario Arts Council–which is an
agency of the Government of Ontario.

 Conseil des Arts
du Canada
Canada Council
for the Arts

 ONTARIO ARTS COUNCIL
CONSEIL DES ARTS DE L'ONTARIO

Published in Canada in 2007 by Exile Editions Ltd.
144483 Southgate Road 14
General Delivery
Holstein, Ontario, N0G 2A0
info@exileeditions.com
www.ExileEditions.com

Canadian Sales Distribution:
McArthur & Company
c/o Harper Collins
1995 Markham Road
Toronto, ON M1B 5M8
toll free: 1 800 387 0117

U.S. Sales Distribution:
Independent Publishers Group
814 North Franklin Street
Chicago, IL 60610
www.ipgbook.com
toll free: 1 800 888 4741

Dedicated to the memory of my grandfather,
John Harold "Pat" Greer, who, after I informed him
I was choosing writing over all other career paths,
finished his cup of tea, lit a cigarette,
and silently left the room.

When he came back, he handed me a Strunk & White.
Thank you, Baba.

CONTENTS

THE DOORKNOB

The bucket held eight bricks, a couple more than Nathan expected, and his booby trap above the front door to his apartment was set. He'd seen this trick played countless times on TV, unsuspecting victims showered with water or confetti. He felt ingenious for his innovation. All that was left to do was test it, and Nathan reached out proudly for the doorknob.

THE ARCADE
SECURITY CAMERA SHOW

Life became rich for Ralph on the day he and Trench and Q-Bert discovered a security camera installed outside the video arcade at the strip mall. Elaborate fight scenes ensued in the parking lot. Ralph always got killed, fake-kicked in the gut when he was down. The boys speculated as to who their audience might be. They howled as their collective imaginations created a zit-popping, potato chip-munching, errant nose hair-plucking, uniform shirt-tucking security guard monitoring black and white TV screens in some concealed office that smelled like egg farts, watching their shows.

Trench and Q-Bert introduced homoeroticism to the show with fake kissing, hands cupped around cheeks, lips close but apart. Accidents happened and sometimes their lips touched. It didn't particularly bother them as long as the camera was on.

One afternoon, Ralph brought some of his sister's dolls. He started a show with Strawberry Shortcake, American Idol Barbie and Veterinarian Barbie living together in an empty 2-litre chocolate milk carton. Ralph explained to Trench and Q-Bert that Veterinarian Barbie and Strawberry Shortcake had syphilis and American Idol Barbie was the only person left willing to care for them, nurse their bed sores and change their Depend undergarments on a regular basis. Q-Bert asked Ralph how he expected to get all that across to the security camera, deaf as it was. "Let's just do a fight," Trench urged. Ralph walked into the Mexican convenience store next to the arcade and bought two pads of typing paper, a black marker and, on a hungry whim, a package of twelve flour tortillas a day past their best before date, half off the regular price.

Outside, he wrote out his first dialogue card and got hot in the earlobes, the choppy fossil of a silent film shown in Social Studies last trimester suddenly not as pathetically laughable as it had seemed. In a remote region inside of Ralph, the germination of something like aspiration, like desire, popped and sizzled for the first time. It felt good, like hunger staring into the face of a breakfast buffet. He approached the camera and held up his card:

HER FRIENDS IN THE FINAL HORRIFYING STAGES

OF SYPHILIS, AMERICAN IDOL BARBIE PLODS ON,

TRYING TO CHOOSE BETWEEN AIR SUPPLY AND

THE GO-GO'S FOR HER FIRST SOLO PERFORMANCE.

Trench and Q-Bert brushed past Ralph. Q-Bert dropped to all fours beneath the camera and Trench stepped up onto his back, balanced, leaped. He dangled, arms draped over the camera, feet kicking air. Q-Bert rose and tugged at Trench's legs until the camera dislodged with a snap and crack of plastic. Q-Bert broke Trench's fall inelegantly, the two bouncing off of each other like Keystone Kops, and the camera crashed to the pavement between them.

"Run!"

In the woods beside the football field, Ralph stuffed stale tortilla into his mouth and watched Trench and Q-Bert bring final destruction to the security camera with a rock and a thick stick. It was still not too late to switch electives for the new trimester, but he'd wait until the deadline had officially passed before informing his buddies he was dropping metal shop for Mr. Hagopian's film study.

NEW

After school Sean found his parents sitting in lawn chairs at the dining room table. Between them lay a package of Whippet cookies, its plastic interior tray removed completely and half empty. Tea steamed from two plastic beer cups. Three brown, slightly water-damaged boxes marked DINING ROOM lined the wall behind his mother's chair. One box had been opened, a few balls of newspaper strewn on the floor before it. Sean announced he was going to see about the Jobs For Students program.

His father, brown spring jacket zipped to his neck, reached for a Whippet and asked how he was getting there.

"Tamara's going. She's bringing me."

"Is that the girl with the hat?" his mother asked too quickly, too enthused.

Sean cringed. "I guess."

Tamara's hat was red and bell-shaped. A thin black band separated the crown and brim. She looked like she was about to board a train in an old movie. Two weeks at the new school and Sean had not once seen Tamara without her hat on.

In the car he stole glances at the stick-shift. That she didn't drive an automatic was a surprise and made him feel worse about not even having his learner's permit yet. Tamara worked the gears mainly with her flattened palm, fingers only glancing over the stick. Her knuckles were thick but her fingertips and nails were skinny. There was lint and flakes of ash caught in the rubber crevices surrounding the stick. Tamara punched the lighter and Sean looked up and ahead. "You want?" she offered. He refused, automatically. But really he did want and regretted saying no but, as they drove, imagined her second-hand smoke was giving him a buzz.

At the employment office there were line-ups and it was hard to tell what each one was for. Tamara said she was going back outside to smoke. "I thought you wanted to sign up, too," Sean said.

"I'll do it another time," she said, adjusting her hat.

After he filled out his forms Sean found Tamara sitting cross-legged on a block of concrete at the edge of the parking lot, three lipstick-stained cigarette butts crunched between her shoes. Her eyes were small but bright, blue. A few freckles dotted her cheeks and her hair was black. Round breasts pushed out and up against a tight charcoal turtleneck. Sean asked if he could have that cigarette now.

After the employment office, in the car, Tamara asked where he hoped to find work. He said anywhere but McDonald's. She said she used to work at McDonald's. He got scared he'd said the wrong thing. She said she wouldn't wish a McDonald's job on her worst enemy, who, she added, happened to be Yvonne Hart. He said he didn't know who that was. She said he'd seen her for sure, noticed her, she dressed like such a slut and wore her pants so low that her butt crack showed all the time, he just didn't know everybody's name yet. He said he still wasn't sure who she was talking about. But he did. Just that morning, outside school before the start of the day, he'd spotted the hair follicles on the small of Yvonne's back, bright blond, almost translucent in the sun.

Tamara downshifted abruptly, shouted the word "coffee" like it was the best idea she'd ever had. She signalled and steered left almost simultaneously, then stalled in front of oncoming traffic. Sean put one hand on the dashboard. Tamara screamed and laughed and got the car going again and lurched forward and stalled again. A horn blasted. Sean laughed. Tamara got the car started again and made it across the road. She slapped Sean's knee twice while they both laughed in the Tim Hortons parking lot. And even before he was finished laughing, Sean was glad it had happened because it was something they could talk about together at school tomorrow and something Sean could talk to other kids about if any other kids talked to him.

Tamara took a couple of wrong turns on the way back to Sean's house. She said she wanted to show him something. They pulled into a driveway, passing a white mailbox decorated with painted-on bluebirds. The driveway was long, and veered right, then left, cutting a path between rows of peeling birch trees. Finally, there was what remained of a house in a big pile of wood, concrete, cinder and ash.

"There was a fire and they tore the place down," Tamara said and one hand went for Sean's seatbelt and the other the button of his pants. She did everything with her hands and didn't even stop when her hat fell off halfway through.

At home Sean found his father crouched behind the television and VCR, sweaty. To be polite, Sean asked him if he was having trouble.

"I can't get it to record one channel while I watch another one. I used to be able to do that. I should be able to do that."

"It is supposed to do that," Sean offered.

"I should be able to do that."

"Any idea yet of when we'll have a fridge by the way?"

The next day at school Sean looked for Tamara at her locker. She was there with her hat on, her back turned, the locker wide open. Two girlfriends flanked her, leaning against neighbouring lockers, arms laden with books. They watched with some confusion as Sean approached. He smiled and tried not to look like a geek at the same time. There were two cartons of cigarettes in Tamara's locker, in plain view, one torn open and short at least two packs. Sean wondered if she always bought in bulk.

He stood there behind her and hoped Tamara would turn around and see him before he had to say anything. The girlfriends stared at him intently. This was the most difficult part of being new, of not being a part of what had happened before. His presence in the hallway was not included in the natural unfolding of events for the girlfriends and the rest of the kids. Except Tamara.

She had taken to him almost immediately. Showed him where the library was. Warned him not to eat the cafeteria food. Introduced him to kids indifferent to him.

Sean decided to come back to her locker after next period when maybe the girlfriends wouldn't be there.

Sean filled the bathtub with water, squeezed out a couple drops of shampoo. He got down on his knees and plunged his socks, underwear, a shirt and a pair of pants into the sudsy water. It smelled like aloe. Tamara had told him about a party coming up on Saturday night and offered a ride. He knew exactly what he wanted to wear but the clothes were dirty. He shook the shirt under the water. His mother poked her head into the bathroom. "You mind if I give you a couple of things to wash?"

"Yes, actually."

"Yes?"

"Yes, actually I mind."

Sean bathed the rest of his outfit. While the tub drained, he rinsed the clothes under running water and wrung them out with strangling fingers. He put all the wet clothes in a plastic grocery bag. Outside, on the back deck, he removed the clothes from the bag and started hanging them on the clothesline, which snapped before the job was complete, cord plunging to the grass. Sean retrieved his clothes from the ground, picked off a few clinging leaves and blades of grass. He went back in the house and reemerged with clothes hangers. He hung his clothes throughout the back yard, from reachable tree branches. When he was done he walked down to the strip mall and bought two singles and smoked them in quick succession standing on the sidewalk between the travel agency and the video store. The thought that he'd like to try lacrosse came to mind.

They walked into the party in the middle of a commotion. Somebody had microwaved an egg and there was a crowd in the kitchen. "This is exactly what I didn't want to happen!" a male voice rang out, shrill. "This'll never clean out!"

Tamara motioned him in the opposite direction. Down a hall, into a room. "Check this out," she said. There were records lined up on the floor, long rows spanning the entirety of two adjoining walls. Tamara sat down on the floor in front of the records, knees up and ankles crossed. She extended a hand and pinched out an album jacket with what, to Sean, unsettlingly, seemed like the familiarity of almost ownership. "They're the older brother's records," she said. Sean felt a very small but very foul burn. "That's a really nice shirt, by the way," Tamara said. "Brown looks awesome on you."

"You know this brother?"

"Check this one out: The B-52's. Sucks there's nothing to play them on."

Sean looked around the room, at anything but the records.

"They didn't try to find another record player when it broke. Kept the records, though."

"You know a lot about them."

"The records?"

"The family." Sean paused. Burned. "The brother."

"So what?"

"I don't know. You friends with him or something?"

Tamara stiffened. "No, actually."

"Cause you have a lot of friends."

"Doesn't mean I fucked them all and I certainly didn't fuck the older brother who's dead by the way if that's what you're getting so fucking nasty about."

"Nasty. Strong word." It was like he couldn't stop himself. There was something unexpectedly enjoyable about the unravelling.

Tamara got up and walked to the door. "I'm going to find a beer. See you." Sean was left to himself in a room full of records with nothing to play them on, in a house full of rooms full of people who didn't talk to him.

Tamara stomped back in just long enough to kick him, hard, in the shin. He watched her stomp back out and whatever had been unravelling was now limp and slack all over the floor.

Sean managed to scrounge a beer in kitchen. He twisted the cap off. It hurt the inside of his thumb slightly. Two drunk girls, laughing their heads off, were helping the host of the party clean out the microwave with what looked like a balled-up, wet T-shirt. They glanced at him briefly, but returned quickly to the molten egg splatter. Sean downed half the beer and decided holding a beer bottle didn't make him feel or, especially, look any less alone. He slipped out the front door.

He walked to the main road and started hitching. He'd never done it before but went about it calmly and deliberately, as if waiting for a bus. Almost immediately, a car slowed and pulled over.

Sean got in the passenger seat beside a man his father's age. Talk radio droned on the radio. Sean told the man he was going anywhere around Gordon Avenue. He withheld his address, lest his mother be waiting hopefully in the window to catch another glimpse of the girl with the hat.

After a few minutes, the man said, "Look at that." He pointed across the passenger side of the front seat, across Sean's field of vision. Sean looked out his window and saw houses, lampposts, a mailbox. Then his left nipple was being squeezed through his brown shirt. He swiped away the hand. The hand squeezed his knee and Sean swatted at it, crossed his legs. "It's okay," the man said. He tried for Sean's stomach. Sean said get the fuck off. Get the fuck off me right now. Sick pig. "It's okay," the man said again. "Come on, it's fun."

Traffic slowed for an intersection and Sean unlatched his seatbelt, opened his door and stepped out onto pavement while the car was still slowly rolling. He left the door swinging open, heard laughter from within the car. For a couple seconds it felt like he was going to fall forward, his weight distribution thrown off, but with some quick steps his feet caught up to his upper half.

He walked home. It took forty minutes. His shin hurt, just enough to notice. He puked twice on the way.

The house was all lit up, every window. Sean opened the front door and stepped inside, something slippery on the carpet beneath his foot. The front room smelled like aloe. A shampoo bottle, plastic cracked, lay at the edge of the carpet. Not far from the bottle the crumpled TV listings from the newspaper, some shows circled, some shows check marked. On the table nearby a plate with an unfinished piece of toast. And there was yelling. His parents. From the next room, the kitchen, maybe the dining room. Maybe both. Words and phrases like godforsaken, shit, asshole, son of a bitch, having a problem, wrong, nuts.

Sean moved to the kitchen doorway. His mother marched into the kitchen through the opposite entrance, from the adjoining dining room. His father was in there, sitting, hands folded on the table, looking ahead at nothing, one foot tapping. In the kitchen his mother loudly scuffed two empty pans around on the stove, haphazard rearrangement. She picked up a bottle of canola oil from the counter, put it right back down with a thump. Opened the utensil drawer and slammed it closed, muffled jangling. Opened and closed it again. She marched back into the dining room. Circled the table. Yelled. More of the same, as before, as all the times before. After two turns of the table she returned to the kitchen and started again with the stovetop.

"Glad you brought all that crap with you guys," Sean said. "Already unpacked it, too."

"Mind your own business," his mother hissed. Slammed the canola oil bottle down.

"Oh, believe me. I will."

Finding Tamara's house took two tries. Two wrong turns and some backtracking before he remembered the right way. All the lights were out except for the front porch. Her car was not in the driveway. Sean sat down in a corner of the front yard, in the darkness, back resting against the trunk of an elm. Waited.

Without a watch and shrouded in darkness, he felt outside of time, outside the world. Waiting under the tree, he was numb. He imagined it as a sneak preview of oblivion.

Sean waited until Tamara reached for her front door handle before saying, "My shin is killing me, you know." Tamara yelped, put one hand on the centre of her chest. She touched the crown of her hat. He watched her walk toward him, stop in front of the tree and fold her arms. "I'm thinking about divorcing my parents and apologizing to you. But not necessarily in that order." He heard her make a short, quiet noise, more than a murmur, less than a grunt. "I'm sorry." Another noise from her. "I'm really sorry. That was bad. That was all me."

Tamara sat down in the grass beside him. "So if you divorce them does that mean you move away?"

"Probably not."

"Probably?"

"Most likely not."

"Take me with you if you do."

"Most definitely yes."

THE IGA KISSING BANDIT

They needed to get Luke done up like a girl because they wanted to get the IGA Kissing Bandit, really fuck him up.

They went to Sylvester's. Everybody knew he was converting his parents' basement into his own salon, preparing to go full tilt into the business just as soon as he got his Cosmetology diploma from the professional program out of the high school.

Sylvester's mother, green robe and no eyebrows, face pale, half-hiding behind the front door, said Sylvester was still in bed. Larry convinced her they were his friends from school, all four of them, and that he wouldn't mind being woken up.

Sylvester didn't bother to change out of his bedclothes, a baby-blue sleeveless T-shirt and grey sweatpants with the waist cord missing, and sleepily escorted the guys down the creaky stairs to the basement. He pissed in the little bathroom down there, listened to them jumping around in his half-finished salon, guys who were certainly not his friends, guys now imploring him to do the job on Luke. He flushed the toilet and scratched his head, dug a crusty sleep crystal from the corner of his left eye.

Somehow, these guys felt it was okay to ask him to do a job on Luke. Even more distressing was the fact that somehow, someway, Sylvester felt it was okay, too. He could hear them beyond the bathroom door, in *his* salon, laughing and mocking him even now, now when they needed him. He turned on the tap but didn't put his hands under the water, out of spite.

With Sylvester in the bathroom, Luke slid into a salon chair installed in the concrete floor of the basement, rested his hangover on squeaky maroon vinyl, and watched the other guys inspect the place. Mikey jumped up, clumsy in Kodiaks, and took hold of a wooden beam in the unfinished ceiling, swung his body and hoisted his legs up, dangled upside-down like a kid on the monkey bars. "You're gonna kill yourself," Larry said. But he lost interest and joined Dean in jeering at the posters and pinups covering three of the walls, all images of men with good hair. Rick Springfield in the early 1980s. Kiefer Sutherland in the late 1980s. Arsenio Hall in the early 1990s. George Clooney in the late 1990s. John Tesh in an indistinguishable era.

Luke swivelled in the salon chair and faced the fourth wall, a floor-to-ceiling mirror with a white melamine shelf installed horizontally along its length, waist-level. He checked his reflection, thought he looked pretty good in his jeans, even sitting. He was happy with the progress of his hair, blond tresses finally beginning to reach his shoulders, knew it would look fabulous in his hockey helmet, and knew to pretend not to know. His eyes looked tired, a little glazed. They'd all had plenty to drink the night before, Luke especially; liquor had helped conceive the plan to get the IGA Kissing Bandit, and more liquor had helped celebrate its conception. He closed his eyes, headache raging, and hoped Sylvester would throw them out, so they could all just forget about it.

The bathroom door opened with an airy sound like an armpit fart, and Luke turned his head, saw Sylvester coming out. Dean hopped over and crouched beside the salon chair, fooled with the levers. There was a click. The chair reclined sharply and violently, giving a little bounce when it reached its limit, with Luke horizontal, his hair giving a little bounce, too. The other guys laughed. Howled. Mikey dropped from the beam, fell on his ass. More howling. Luke giggled, too. He saw Sylvester march over, disappear behind him, and with a quick jerk Luke was sitting up straight again. He felt like he was in a dentist's chair. Sylvester was reflected in the mirror, professional-looking behind the chair. Stubble dotted his face, heavier in the moustache area; he looked angry, peering over the top of Luke's head. Luke searched for other things for his eyes to look at and found the toes of his running shoes in the mirror beneath the shelf. On the shelf between a hairdryer and a jar full of scissor and combs, a little clock radiated 9:49 AM in red digital characters.

Larry pulled a wad of bills rolled up with a red rubber band from his jeans pocket, waved it at Sylvester. "So how much is this going to cost us?" Ten seconds of silence. "We're going to *pay* you," he said defensively.

They pulled into the IGA parking lot a little before noon, all of them bouncing around in Dean's mom's forest-green Windstar, Luke amazed they'd come this far. The plan was a good joke, a scenario to laugh about. Even while he was in Sylvester's chair, looking up at pink skin tags scattered among the future beautician's brown armpit hairs, he kept waiting for somebody to call it off. And even after the makeover was complete, he didn't think they'd actually go to the grocery store. But here they were, backing the minivan into a parking spot near the back of the lot, with an unobstructed view of the store's entrance and exit doors.

The cackling was wild, fever-pitched, when the IGA Kissing Bandit finally emerged with a customer, a pudgy woman wearing a purple sweatsuit; she was in her early fifties, with black curly hair and huge sunglasses. The Kissing Bandit had his green IGA windbreaker on, unzipped, grocery apron showing under it. He was probably twenty-five years old, dark stubble high on his cheeks. Short black hair standing up straight in the front, gelled like a pro. A light brown birthmark on his left temple. He followed the woman to a section of the parking lot off to the right of the minivan, one brown paper grocery bag and a jumbo box of laundry detergent nestled in his cart.

"What a skank," Larry scoffed from the passenger seat in the front. Luke laughed. He was pressed up against the side window in the back, Mikey behind him trying to get a good look outside. The tissues and cotton balls that stuffed Luke's bra mingled with the hairs on his chest, tickled him.

"Doesn't matter," Mikey said, straining to look over Larry's shoulder, practically humping him in the excitement. "He'll do it. Skank or no skank. He'll do it no matter what."

The purple-sweatsuit lady pointed to her car, and her purse strap slid off her shoulder, down her arm. She opened the purse with her other hand – maybe the whole motion had been on purpose, Luke speculated. Or maybe the strap had simply slipped. Luke wondered which it was, felt he should know the answer for sure before heading out himself. It might be important.

The woman opened the back of a light-blue Chevette. The Kissing Bandit put the detergent in first, then the paper grocery bag. He raised one arm in the air, clasped the hatch with his fingers. The lady reached out with a closed fist toward the Bandit, in offering – obviously money, but it was impossible to see how much. The Bandit's other arm went straight out, palm up and outstretched, a gentle snatch. A quick deposit into his apron pocket and he looked to one side, the other, the first side once more, and then his head bobbed forward like it was popping out of the water doing the breaststroke, and his lips were on purple sweatsuit lady's lips. The Windstar exploded with a cheer, the boys jumping up and down, whacking each other like caged monkeys. After a few high-fives, a couple of hoots, and some considerable pounding on the back of the front seat's headrest, Luke glanced toward the Chevette again. The hatchback was closed, the Bandit was pushing his cart back to the IGA entrance, and the lady was fumbling with her car keys without actually looking at them. Her head was motionless, fixed in a straight-ahead stare, dazed.

The guys started chanting his name. "Luke! Luke! Luke! Luke!" It was actually going to happen. Larry turned around and handed him the remainder of the cash, the red rubber band a little slack now. When they had put the funds together at Dean's the night before, all the guys throwing money into an old Black Hawks hat while the spliff made the rounds of the room, Luke didn't think it was really going to happen. Even when he agreed to be the mark, his long blond hair making him a natural for the role, Luke had no doubt the plan would fall apart. It was ambitious, too ambitious, yet typical of their sauced imaginations, and he put his twenty bucks in the cap confident they would wind up spending the money on more beer and more grass the next night.

Larry pushed the cash into his hand. "There's still enough for a two-four, but get other stuff, too – broccoli, meat – make it look good. Make it look real."

To Luke there was little more real than the erection that had been on almost constantly under his skirt since his first glance at himself all done up in Sylvester's mirror.

He stumbled out the minivan's sliding side door, feeling his friends' encouraging slaps on his shoulders and back. He strategically placed Dean's mother's old purse before his crotch and turned to face the guys one last time before going in. Larry lit a cigarette and tossed the burnt match out the front passenger window. "Remember," he said, a little cloud of smoke with each syllable, "we're right here. Right behind you. Make it look good. Do your part and leave the rest to us." Luke nodded and turned, made for the IGA entrance. He stumbled a bit in his heels.

It was a cool day, mid-October, grey sky. Orange and yellow leaves whipped by his feet, carried by a crisp wind. Many long and boring school weeks still lay ahead, but Christmas vacation was kind of coming up. Luke held the image of his own snow-swept street, his house and his neighbours' lit up for the holidays, until his hard-on began to deflate.

Sylvester sat in the back of the Windstar, behind the driver's seat, his legs and arms crossed. He concentrated on staying quiet, making himself small, invisible. He didn't want to be there. But when they asked him to come along he'd said yes automatically. He was ashamed now for the gratitude he'd felt at the invitation. He didn't want to be there but somehow couldn't get himself to leave. Couldn't move.

Larry turned around and leaned into the backseat area. "Y'wanna a smoke, girly man?" he asked, extending his pack. Sylvester reached for a cigarette impulsively, feeling that gratitude he hated again, said thank you as sarcastically as he could muster, and accepted Larry's match. He blew smoke out his nostrils and looked at the road beside the IGA parking lot. Cars passed, the trees were bare, grey swirls of smoke escaped chimneys of houses. He tried to follow the road with his eyes as far away as he could.

Luke spied his own reflection in the big window next to the automatic doors and slowed for a closer look. He got excited fast; a quick intake of breath, a shiver all over. It was maddening, confusing, but he couldn't look away. He was so convincing. Black low heels (still feeling quite high to him) that his feet had slipped into with surprising ease. Black skirt, the hem well above the knees, a good portion of thigh showing. White blouse, long sleeved because he had been willing to shave his legs but not his arms, with small, gold-coloured buttons outlined in black, done up to the top to play it safe. The Kleenex and cotton balls, however, gave him a beautiful pair of breasts with, thanks to Sylvester's diligence, a slight upward curve, not too small and not too big. "Just perfect for kneadin' and rollin'," Dean had joked, almost too lavishly, as the guys looked him over in Sylvester's basement. And Luke felt bad for all the times he'd called Sylvester names, to his face and behind his back, because faggot or not he had done an amazing job.

His blond hair was pinned flat in the front with pink and purple barrettes; in back it curled out slightly on both sides. His makeup was subtle, realistic – just a dash of lipstick, a dusting of mascara, nothing overdone. He twisted slightly and nonchalantly inspected his ass in the black skirt. He felt sexy. His erection pressed his underwear taut. Along with arousal, however, came an eerie sense of grief, a deep burn in the base of his throat. Somehow, as he stood there staring at the girl in the reflection, admiring her, he was also mourning her. Mourning a girl who had not died but who would never live. A girl he would never meet and who would never meet him, not without the barrier of reflective glass between them, never to touch, to connect. Shielded behind the purse, Luke passed through the automatic doors and into the IGA.

He caught his first stare early in the vegetable aisle. It was an ugly guy dressed all in blue denim, red baseball cap and bristly stubble dotting flabby cheeks and a double chin, loading up on the complimentary coffee. Swizzle stick stuffed in the corner of his mouth like an old cigar, white crud on his bottom lip, his face lit up as Luke pushed his empty shopping cart past him. Without even looking back, Luke could feel the twin laser beams of the guy's stare trained on his hips and ass, hated and loved it at the same time.

Sylvester asked Mikey to slide the side door open and he tossed his smoked cigarette outside. "Actually," he announced, "you know what, guys? I gotta go. Thanks for everything, but I gotta get home."

"Whoa!" Dean said, turning around in the driver's seat. He motioned to Mikey with his chin and the sliding door was quickly shut. "Don't you wanna see if it works? This is, like, your work on the line, man. Don't you wanna see what happens?"

I'm afraid of what's going to happen, Sylvester thought. He crossed his legs and made himself small in the back seat again.

In the cereal aisle, Luke took to swaying his hips slightly with each step. The skirt slid gently up and down his thighs, barely an inch each way, seemingly designed for this kind of motion. Not only men but women were checking him out now. Mere glances from the front, fleeting and subtle, but from behind the stares were searing. Luke glanced back once in a while to watch the ladies look down or away quickly, embarrassed.

He reached for a box of Cheerios and tossed it in his cart. It looked lonely in there with the broccoli. He reminded himself to make it all look real. He added a box of Frosted Mini Wheats. At the end of the cereal aisle he caught a man his father's age ogling his legs. Impulsively, Luke raised his skirt a little, pretended to scratch an itch on his left thigh. His admirer whistled exaggerated appreciation. Luke blushed.

He turned his cart right, right again, up the pasta and cake mix aisle. He increased the sway in his hips just a bit. Leaning his arms on the shopping cart handle and pushing it forward at the same time, he turned to see the man following, smiling with his eyes half closed, conspiratorially, unafraid to look right at him. Then a "Look out!" from in front, and there he was, the IGA Kissing Bandit.

He cradled a stack of dented tomato sauce cans with his arms and chest, steadied it with his chin. "Almost had a collision there," the Bandit said with a smile. Then a wink. "I'll see you later?" Another wink and a sideways nod of the head at Luke's shopping cart. Luke silent. Heart in his throat. Dampness in his armpits. Heat on the back of his neck. Couldn't stop staring at the Bandit's lips. Dry-looking, not much darker than the skin on his face. A cramp low down in Luke's stomach. He pushed his cart forward, felt the IGA Kissing Bandit's stare, but he didn't dare look back.

"What's taking him so long?" Larry asked nobody in particular, frustrated, feet up on the dashboard. He lit another cigarette. "It's not that complicated, groceries. Let's get this show on the road for fuck's sake."

Sylvester took a deep breath. "What exactly is going to happen? You guys have some kind of a plan?"

Larry turned his head, smoke escaping his mouth like a fog. "Oh, yeah. We got a plan." He high-fived Dean. Mikey chortled. Sylvester looked at the road again.

Luke was fourth in line at one of the cash registers, and he saw the IGA Kissing Bandit leave the store with a tall woman's groceries in his cart. "Bitch," he couldn't help but think. He was happy, though, felt the timing was just right for him to wind up with the Bandit.

But it wasn't, not exactly. The lady in front of him, perhaps sixty years old, with an order consisting mainly of tuna fish cans and frozen vegetables, was ready to leave when the Bandit returned to the store. The Bandit began walking toward her, automatically. He even started to smile at her. Luke stared at him while loading his groceries on the rubber conveyer belt. The Bandit's eyes met his. Luke shivered at what seemed unsaid. The Bandit squeezed by the old lady and helped Luke lift a case of Molson Dry from the shopping cart to the conveyer belt. "See you in a minute," the Bandit whispered, then disappeared up the bread aisle.

Luke dug into the bottom of Dean's mom's old purse. It was empty save for the roll of bills with the red rubber band. He was short two dollars. He asked the cashier to remove the Frosted Mini Wheats from his order. He was owed change. A nervous-looking teenager with a single shiny red zit on his chin bagged Luke's groceries, paid Luke little heed. The stares of others, however, customers and employees, were undeniable. His order all set to go, and the Kissing Bandit appeared, seemingly out of nowhere. A wink. Luke fell in beside him like it was something he did every day, matched his steps and listened to his small talk. Smiled. Shrugged. Glanced.

"Okay! Here they come, Jesus fuck! Hide!" Dean shrieked. Mikey jumped up on the back seat, crouched and held his knees, bayed like a dog. Larry told them both to shut up.

Sylvester craned his neck to see out the front windshield. He felt proud and sick. Luke was stunning. The IGA Kissing Bandit could not keep his eyes off him. Sylvester was more confident in his abilities in that moment than ever before. This was better than a diploma in Cosmetology. This was real life. And that's what made him sick. The *real life* part.

Luke pointed to the Windstar. He tried to make his voice soft. "Over there." He looked down, smiled, stole a glance at the Kissing Bandit. The Kissing Bandit winked again. Luke stared at his lips. He had to avoid them. The guys had to act before it happened. They'd promised.

The Kissing Bandit asked Luke his name. "Lucy," he replied.

"You live around here, Lucy?"

"In the new development behind the mall," Luke invented. The Bandit asked Lucy if she was new to town, then. Luke cleared his throat and answered yes, she was. The Bandit told Lucy about the great new inline skating rink and adjoining movie theatre down on Lobo Road. Luke said, "Wow," half-expecting to be asked to the entertainment complex on a date, half-disappointed when he wasn't.

Luke directed the Kissing Bandit to the back of the Windstar. He opened the hatch. "You really should keep that locked you know," the Bandit said, mock scolding, a wink and a smile. Luke smiled back. The Bandit placed the groceries in the van, one bag at a time, buffering them finally with the case of beer. They closed the hatch together.

"Okay, it's closed," Larry whispered from the floor of the front seat. "What're they doing?"

Mikey peered over the back seat, not raising more than his eyes above the vinyl. "They're just standing there. Looking at each other."

"Well," Luke said, pausing. "Thank you very much."

"You're welcome," the Bandit said, magnanimously. He clasped his hands together and rested them at the centre of his waist, looked down and to the side.

"Well. Thanks again." Luke took a step forward. He dropped his eyes, shyly. He looked up, utterly uncertain of what to do. He had to get the Bandit to try and kiss him. That was the plan. The Bandit goes for it and the boys jump him. He had to get him to make a move.

"Well," Luke said again. He looked shyly at the ground. "Um," he laughed nervously. "Um, aren't you going to –?"

The Bandit cleared his throat. Luke looked up. The Bandit bobbed his chin, pointed with it at the purse. He raised one eyebrow, waiting. Luke's erection rested against the side of the purse, out of sight. He reached into it carefully, never moving it from its place. He extracted the change. Two dollars and six cents. He handed it to the Bandit.

"Thank you very much and it was nice meeting you, Lucy." The Bandit walked backward against his cart, pushing it along, waving bye-bye.

"But—"

"Just so you know," the Bandit said, hushed, checking around, "you're about eight bucks short of, um, the VIP treatment." He puckered his lips and kissed the air, winked. "See you next time." He turned around and placed his left foot on the lower bar of his cart, pushed off repeatedly with his right foot, rolled back to the IGA as if on a scooter. As he neared the entrance he stepped up with his right foot, rode his momentum, then leaned his body a little to the right, and the cart turned accordingly. The IGA Kissing Bandit disappeared back into his store. A grey-haired lady with a single plastic grocery bag dangling from her hand paused in the doorframe to watch him go by.

The guys poured out of the Windstar. Larry kicked the parking lot pavement. Dean said, "Fuck." Mikey burped and said, "Fuck," too. Sylvester poked his head out the open side door. Luke felt his erection fade.

"What the hell happened? What did you do?" Dean asked him.

"It costs like ten fucking bucks to get him to kiss. I didn't know!"

"Then why didn't you give it to him for Christ's sake?"

"I didn't have enough!"

"Aw, shit. This fucking sucks." Dean dug into his pocket. Came away with lint and a dime. "This really sucks. You guys got any money?"

"Forget it, Dean," Luke said. "Let's get out of here." He put the purse on the ground – it was safe to let go of it now – started undoing his blouse buttons, anxious to get to his real clothes in the car.

"Don't do that out here," Sylvester advised from the van.

"Who asked you to talk, you stupid fuck?" Dean barked, approaching Sylvester with a sidestep, his chest out, as if he'd been challenged to a fight. "Fucking faggot. Nobody told you to talk, nobody cares what you have to say."

"Leave him alone, Dean," Luke said, tired. Tired of it all.

"You gonna let that faggot tell you what to do?" Dean shot back, seemingly ready to fight Luke now. He grabbed his crotch and his voice came out overdone falsetto: "*Don't do that out here.*" He skipped closer to Sylvester, started sparring. Sylvester cowered, punches whistling past his ears, each one closer than the last. The other guys laughed. Luke's hangover returned with renewed and stifling vigour.

"I'm telling you, Dean, just leave him the fuck alone."

"*Somebody's* ass is gonna get whupped today," Dean sang, his tone somewhere between gangster movie and professional wrestling interview. He started cuffing the sides of Sylvester's head, softly at first but with growing intensity. "Supposed to be the IGA Kissing fuckin' Bandit, but I'll beat on this candy ass if I have to."

Luke stopped working at getting his blouse off. He walked over to the scuffle and got behind Dean. He inserted both forearms under Dean's armpits, linked his fingers behind Dean's neck – full nelson applied – and lurched his buddy up and away from Sylvester. "I said leave him alone," Luke grumbled, releasing the hold.

"You looking to get your ass kicked now?" Dean challenged. "Eh, fuckup?"

Luke turned and walked away from Dean, toward the minivan. Mikey and Larry were already climbing in, climbing past Sylvester. Luke outstretched his hand. "Somebody wanna give me my clothes?"

Dean blindsided him waist-high with a hip check, and he was down on all fours on the parking lot pavement, right knee and elbow stinging. He looked up and saw Sylvester being pulled from the back seat of the minivan, a look of utter shock on his face, Dean depositing him unflatteringly on the ground.

"The two of you can have a good old time and fuck each other up the ass," Dean spat, dismissing them as he hopped into the driver's seat. He started up the engine and called out the open window: "Get the fucking Bandit to join in – make it a three-way, you fucking faggots." He peeled out, tires shrieking.

Luke got himself to his feet, watched Dean's mom's minivan lurch out of the parking lot, wheel up the street. "My clothes?" he yelled, in vain. "Assholes."

He offered Sylvester a hand to get up off the ground. They said little to each other as they walked back to their part of the neighbourhood. Along the way the blisters started, so Luke took the low heels off and continued barefoot. The forest-green minivan returned, slowing abreast of them, horn bleating, the cackling resonating,

Mikey hanging out the front passenger window with a camcorder, Larry in the back window with a moon.

"Nice ass," Sylvester offered, deadpan, only loud enough for Luke to hear.

Luke chuckled. He adjusted his skirt, pulled it taut. Checked himself out and smiled. "Not as nice as mine, I'll tell you that much. Not as nice as mine."

LOST DOG

I slip my sunglasses on halfway up the escalator. At the top, it's bright. Windows tall as the ceiling is high at street level, the sunlight pouring in. People squinting. Rushing from the Métro station to the buses outside.

I head for the line-up for the 175. Spot my friend Horse third from the front. We'll have seats this morning. Everybody has messy speech balloons of steam funnelling out their mouths and noses in the cold. I pull out a cigarette and make a cup of my hands to light it. I probably look like a chimney stack.

Horse has earphones in. Little white buds. My hands in my jacket pockets, I nudge him with an elbow. He sees me, frees up one of his ears. Makes some room for me to cut in.

"What are you listening to?"

"Crash Test Dummies."

I've known Horse almost all my life. It's amazing how little I know about him. "You still listen to them?"

End of the summer, 1991, my Dairy Queen job at Laronde had just finished for the year. There were a few days left before school started up. A second exhilarating year of undergraduate Poly Sci studies at McGill awaited me. I was outside on the terrace of a bar, sucking back beers with Horse and our other buddy Shift.

"So who's playing tonight?" Shift asked.

"The Crash Test Dummies," I answered, nodding my head toward Sainte Catherine Street. The concert venue was just down a ways.

"The Crash what?"

"Crash Test Dummies."

"You know," Horse jumped in, "they sing that *Superman's Song* song." Then he sang a line, the part about Superman not making any money saving the world from Solomon Grundy.

This got Shift and I cackling. We were working on our fourth pitcher. Things were going down smooth and easy. In our inebriated state, we were like little kids who'd been tickled so much that just the movement of hands toward our bellies, without even actually touching, could set us off laughing. Just waiting for the next tickle, like Horse singing *Superman's Song*. Doing his best to imitate the Crash Test Dummies' lead singer's deep, guttural voice, even though his own was high-pitched and whiny.

Horse was good for that sort of thing. No matter what was going on, he could always be counted upon to make a fool of himself at some point. Shift and I laughed at him, in an exaggerated, drunken sort of way. Horse laughed a little bit, too. He always took the teasing well, especially when we were drunk. We probably would have laughed at his singing had we been sober, too, only I wouldn't have drooled beer all over my lap while doing it.

The bus is late arriving. I offer Horse a smoke from my pack. He refuses, taps out one of his own.

"Since when do you smoke menthols?"

"I've got a cold."

Horse and I work at the same place. His Dad has a lighting company. Horse puts stuff up on the company's shitty website and, for all

I know, surfs the net and drinks coffee the rest of the day. I work in shipping. Every Monday morning, us warehouse stiffs perform this ritual in the lunchroom. Earl Tutton, a forklift driver and only 30-year man still with the company, walks in a little before the bell goes off and yells out, "Monday again!" Then Daniel Fillion, my supervisor in shipping, replies, "Another Monday means there's another Friday coming up!"

I used to laugh at those guys. Pathetic warehouse lifers. But now I take part. There's been a recent addition to the Monday morning ceremony. After Daniel reminds us all about Friday's inevitable arrival, everybody raises their styrofoam coffee cups and says, "To Wilf!" It's a tribute to Wilfred Caron who died last fall of a heart attack after 36 years in the packaging department. I had never seen a dead person before I saw Wilf lying on the warehouse floor, his right hand clutching a staple gun. Of course, I didn't know he was actually dead at the time, what with everybody crowding around, saying, "Hang in there, Wilf." And, "He'll be okay. Just wait and see."

A couple days later a few of us were slacking off, kicking the tires of a forklift, out of sight between some of the tall, dusty inventory shelves in the warehouse. One of the guys said he heard that the doctors at the hospital had to use medical pliers to pry the staple gun from Wilf's dead stiff hand. I laughed. "What the fuck are *medical* pliers?" The looks the other guys gave me. You'd have thought I'd just pissed on Wilf's grave. Now I make sure to be nice and vocal Monday mornings.

The night of the Crash Test Dummies show was back in the days when Boreale beer was new. Horse was having flatulence problems that particular evening. He attempted to blame it on the beer. "Can't we just order Molson?"

"Molson makes you fart, too," Shift said. "Breathing makes you fart."

Microbrewery beer was pretty novel to us then. We tried out the Boreale Rousse (Shift said, "Red beer? What the fuck?"), and we tried the Blonde. Finally, we went in on the Dark. The Boreale Dark was definitely dark, and thick as molasses, too. Shift couldn't drink it. Made him gag. I liked it. Horse pretended to like it.

Shift suggested we get some cigarettes. I thought he'd never ask. We all put our coins on the table and Shift got up to buy a pack from the machine near the bathrooms inside the bar. I had been dying for a cigarette all night, but I hadn't come out as a smoker yet. Hadn't really admitted it to myself yet.

We all lit up smokes. Horse had this ridiculous way of doing it. He held the cigarette in one hand and touched a burning match to the end of it. Then he stuck the cigarette in his mouth all quick before it went out. Took him two tries before it took.

"What the hell do you do it like that for?"

"The smoke burns my eyes when I light it in my mouth."

"Baby."

I took a deep haul into my lungs and followed up with a big gulp of Boreale Dark before exhaling the smoke. I got a big buzz off of that.

"There is nothing quite so sweet as dragging on a cigarette after knocking back a few beers," Shift proclaimed. Horse and I muttered agreement. But I saw through Shift's little comment. It was just a fancy way of saying, re-stating actually, because he said it all the time, that he'd never smoke sober. As if it was only safe to do it when drinks were involved. He was in denial about his smoking. I knew he was because I was, too. If he was at all like me he was smoking away in his off-drinking hours and just not telling anybody about it. If it made Shift more comfortable to call himself a social smoker, I wasn't going to call him on it or anything. In that moment, however, I knew I was hooked and hooked good. A tiny part of me cared.

I looked at my watch. "Hey," I said. "Maybe we should head over soon. The show's supposed to start at eight."

"There's no rush." Shift grabbed the half-empty pitcher of Dark from the table and held it in the air, seeking the waitress' attention. "Who's opening?"

"Some band called the Barenaked Ladies."

Horse giggled. "Naked ladies."

"Are you serious?" Shift snorted.

I nodded. "That's what it said in the *Mirror*."

"Is it a chick band?" Shift asked.

"I seriously doubt it. But let's go and we'll find out."

"Whoever they are," Shift said, "they probably suck. They're the opening act. Let's wait a while longer. And besides, George told me he might be coming by. Let's see if he wants to go, too."

Oh great, I thought. George might be coming by.

Horse is being his usual dreary self at the bus stop. Nothing to say. Various combinations of grass, hash, beer and snack fare keeps our friendship alive. We meet up once or twice a week after work to get high and watch movies from his preposterously large collection of personally pirated VHS tapes. *Total Recall, Twister, Die Hard with a Vengeance*, stuff like that. He was so fucking proud of himself in the '90s for owning two VCRs.

The familiar silence between the two of us is disrupted by a weird clicking sound. Like a clock out of whack. I check around and see what I take at first to be a wolf, but it's a black German Shepherd, rambling along the side of the road across from the bus line.

The dog rolls at a speed somewhere between a walk and a run, paws clicking away on the pavement. Its head down, moving from side to side, nose in constant exploration of the ground. Its tongue dangles out the left side of its mouth, a cloud of white steam blowing out its snout. He moves with effortless fluidity and purpose, and yet, despite the speed, doesn't seem to be in any particular hurry to get anywhere.

"That's a lost dog," Horse says.

I'm not so sure.

The dog wears no collar, but a red checkered scarf is fastened around its neck. Filthy and torn, hanging on like a foggy memory of the dexterous hands that tied the knot who knows how long ago. Also in disrepair is the dog's tail. It bends the wrong way. Sharp burrs attached to it like parasites. He looks like he just emerged from battle, be it with another animal or with a nasty patch of shrubbery. I wince at the thought of how badly his tail must hurt, but the dog never seems to stop wagging it.

George Whitney was a new friend of Shift's, somebody he'd met in his Management class. They did a project together. All through it we heard constantly about was how cool this guy was. I finally got my first glimpse of George when I ran into him and Shift on the crowded steps of the Arts Building. I was wearing my Rush shirt, the one I bought at the Forum during the *Presto* tour. Shift introduced us. George pointed at my shirt. "Nice bunnies. Rush? Those guys still exist?"

I hated what he said, and I hated the way his curled-up, astonished lips caused two small dimples to form on his perfect, zitless cheeks. Even more, however, I hated that Shift said nothing. Just smiled and stayed silent. Even though he owned the very same

T-shirt, and had bought it on the very same night that I bought mine.

I suddenly felt fat. My shirt fit me tighter than it used to. I had been pounding back shish taouks for weeks and it was showing. I tried to stay cool, though. "Yeah, they're still around. They exist."

George started playing a set of air drums, crashed and banged on imaginary cymbals, tapped his foot. This made the other students hanging out on the steps laugh. Without moving his head, George looked around with his eyes, obviously checking that he com-manded everyone's full attention before he made his next joke. "Yeah, Rush! Yeah!" He pumped his fist and sang a line from *Suite Madame Blue*, exaggerated dramatics. Gaze in your looking glass and all that.

"Um," I interrupted, "that's a Styx song."

All those other students started to laugh again. Louder. At first I thought they were laughing at George. But a couple of them were pointing at me. Even Shift had a nasty smirk on his face. It seemed George could do no wrong. I slung my backpack over my shoulder. "Catch you later, Shift."

Walking away, I heard George ask nobody in particular, "Shift? Who the hell is Shift?"

The guys at work call me Tea, and I don't even drink it. But I use the kettle in the staff lunchroom. I love a cup of weak black coffee. I found that out by accident. Screwed up the measurements when I made a pot at home one time and never went back. Before work and on breaks I pour myself half a cup of hot kettle water, the other half coffee.

First time Jimmy Ledwidge, this fat forklift driver, saw me do it he asked if I was making tea. Before I could answer he goes and says,

"'Cause we don't want any tea-drinking faggots around here, eh?" That elicited guffaws from most of the lunchroom.

"You put cream in your coffee?" I hissed back.

"Yup."

"Well I put hot water. I don't go in much for the cream, if you know what I mean."

The lunchroom erupted. Jimmy looked pissed but after that he left me alone. One little victory for me, but the Tea name has dogged me ever since.

To Horse, I am still Taurus, the nickname I acquired in the mid '80s when my mom started driving the car of the same name. Shift earned his nickname in more glorious fashion, in Grade 7 English class. We were reviewing vocabulary words, had to use them in sentences. When it was his turn, he read out: "The shift really hit the fan when the students set the teacher's desk on fire." We all thought it was hilarious. Mrs. Adams, not so much. Shift got detention for the afternoon and a nickname for life.

Growing up, we socialized with guys with names like Pinhole, General Rudeness, Measles, and Le Grand. Most everyone's given name was abandoned at some point, and not always for easily memorable reasons. Horse, however, made it all the way through elementary school and nearly through the end of high school without a nickname. He felt left out and complained about it all the time. "I want a nickname. Somebody, give me a nickname." Over and over. Somewhere along the line, Shift said he was like that song, *Horse With No Name.* Horse was so disappointed when he realized that had stuck.

"Looks like he's been in a few fights," Horse offers.

Everybody in line for the bus is watching the dog now. Slender and solidly built, eyes sharp and aware, dark as its fur. It turns suddenly from its course and crosses to our side of the street. A bus with an Hors Service/Out of Service sign in its front window screeches to avoid hitting it. The dog hops onto the sidewalk without missing a click, and turns, continuing in his original direction. Now an older bald man with a white Poodle on a leash stands in the German Shepherd's path. The man pulls his dog off the sidewalk, out of the way. The Shepherd pays no attention. Strolls right by the spot they had been standing on.

The dog reaches the end of the bus and Métro area and turns south on Decarie Boulevard. The same way the 175 goes. I watch until the dog is out of sight. The morning entertainment seemingly over.

"Think I should call the police? Animal control?" Horse asks.

"What for?"

"It's a lost dog." He's got his cell phone out.

"Lost from where? Did that dog look like it belonged to anybody?"

"Loose dog, then. Dog on the loose."

"Oooo. Real scary." The 175 pulls around the corner. I take a last haul off my smoke and crush it under my boot. "Just forget it. If he was dangerous he would have eaten that poodle. Leave it alone."

Horse returns his phone to his jacket pocket. The blue and grey metal hull of the 175 slows and stops before me. Before climbing on I take a last glimpse over where the dog disappeared. There are at least five people in line behind us on their phones. I hope Horse is the only busybody among us.

I discovered shish taouk pitas early on in my first year of university. Ache-starving for a drunken midnight snack one night, me and the guys were walking toward Burger King when, through the window of a little Middle Eastern fast food place, we caught sight of three incredibly large masses of meat rotating on skewers. "Check out the carcasses," Shift said, pointing. "Let's eat THAT." For three white suburban kids loose and smashed on the streets of Montreal, it was a novelty too good to pass up. Inside, we read the poster menu on the wall. Shawarma came close, but shish taouk pitas sounded like the most ridiculous thing to order. I almost wept it was so delicious. I went back to the counter and ordered a second one while still chewing the last bite of my first.

After that I spent a lot of breaks in the school day heading over to Parc Avenue for a shish taouk or two. I'd snake through all the little streets of the McGill Ghetto, ducking in and out of the back alleys that ran behind the apartments, smoking all the time, hoping but mainly knowing nobody that I knew would see me. Discovering shish taouk did a lot of good for my taste buds. Expanded my food horizons. And, along with it, my waistline. I put on nearly 15 pounds between September and March. I usually went to this place called, appropriately enough, Taouk. Behind the counter was Mahmoud, who liked to tease me because I once asked, naively, for extra beets, not realizing the sweet slices of purple vegetable they garnished their sandwiches with were in fact pickled turnips.

There was this one day during mid-terms. I was walking back to school from Taouk, eating a pita on my way, eager to return to the library with an exam on the British Parliament later on in the afternoon. And who do I see across the street but George Whitney, strolling along in the opposite direction. He was alone, no groupies in tow like Shift and the other pricks who laughed at me outside the Arts Building. I assumed he was on his way to his place. Shift had told all about the "way cool" condo that George's parents had set him up with in the La Cité complex. And he didn't look like he was expecting to see anybody he knew, or for anybody he knew to see him, because he was picking his nose in plain sight. Really digging for gold.

I was worried he'd catch me staring at him from the other side of the street, but I couldn't take my eyes off of him. George had his right index finger stuck halfway up his right nostril. He twisted his finger back and forth in little semi-circles. He pulled his finger out of his nose, inspected it, then thrust his thumb into the same nostril. He made a few flicking motions with his thumb, extracting it once in a while to look at it. I hoped that, if he ever got the snot out, he'd eat it. It seemed petty, even at the time, but it was a strangely empowering experience. I felt so differently than the way I did the first time I met him on campus. I wished somebody, mainly Shift, had been with me to witness the infallible George Whitney picking his nose.

George and I came abreast of each other and I turned my head to keep watching him. I took an inattentive bite of my shish taouk. The expression on George's face changed suddenly from intense focus to happiness and relief. He had finally hauled something out – I could tell because he kept flicking his thumb and index finger together. It must have been pretty sticky.

I was extremely tempted to yell something across the street. I should have. Something sarcastic and sharp. Like, "Hey, George! Need a fork?" Or, "Pick a winner, dude!" I couldn't bring myself to do it. Somehow, it seemed inappropriate. As if I didn't have the right. It's weird, though, because I could imagine him yelling worse stuff than that at me if I had been the one caught picking my nose. I should have said something, should have done something to at least let him know that I'd seen him picking. I was so distracted I walked right into a mailbox. I lost my grip on my shish taouk. It tumbled from my hand and rolled off the slanted mailbox top, down to the ground, leaving a messy trail of tahini and shredded lettuce in its wake. By the time I straightened myself out, George was gone from sight. I don't think I'd ever felt so grateful than at that moment, to know I hadn't been seen.

Horse and I board the bus and grab a seat together near the front. Horse on the window side, headphones in both ears again. I spot an abandoned sports section from today's *La Presse* on the seat across the aisle from us and grab it before anybody else does. I flip through the pages, checking first for anything written by François Gagnon, settle in with his latest dispatch from the Canadiens' road trip.

The bus fills up quickly, the aisle jammed with people who have no seats to sit in. Packed to the hilt, the bus starts up, jerks forward. I've got somebody's butt right beside my ear so I shift a couple centimetres closer to Horse. He glances at me for a second, then turns to the window.

I lose myself in thoughts of hockey as the bus slows and stops, accelerates, slows and stops again. I think about the nachos I'll eat and the beers I'll drink in front of the TV tonight, Canadiens at Buffalo. I weigh the pros and cons of inviting Horse over. If I provide him with nachos and beer, he'll likely bring along his bong. Thing is, I don't particularly like watching hockey with him. He doesn't possess any substantial hockey knowledge yet bitches and moans when the Canadiens play poorly. Plus he doesn't like olives and claims to be allergic to mushrooms, seriously limiting the garnish options for my nachos. He usually goes home by the second intermission, though. Right when I'm hankering for a second batch.

Horse nudges me. "Looks like they're going to get that lost dog."

The bus is stopped at a red light. I check through Horse's window, scan around, spot the dog in the parking lot of a McDonald's. A bright yellow plastic garbage bag lies torn at its feet, old cheeseburgers and hamburgers still in their wrappers spilling out from within. The dog's snout sifts through the trash. I smile to myself and think what a smart dog this is. He's chewing, paper and all, steam puffing out from between his jaws in the cold air. I sink when Horse points to the far end of the parking lot.

Two men in matching navy blue jumpsuits are making their way from the front of a white city pickup to the rear. One of them lets the tailgate down. There's a large cage sitting on the truck bed and the worker opens it up. Then he reaches for something, hands the other guy a pair of oversized gloves. The first one reaches back into the truck bed and comes away with a long metal stick with a thick plastic lasso attached to the end of it. It looks one of those lifeguard poles from a swimming pool. They begin to stroll calmly but steadily toward the dog.

The waitress brought more Boreale Rousse, the plastic pitcher dripping little beads of beer sweat. Shift filled Horse's glass, but insisted on emptying the dregs of the pitcher of Dark into mine since I was the one who wanted it in the first place. I was getting hungry. I checked my watch. "If we want to get a shish taouk before the show we better get a move on after this one."

"Quit freaking," Shift said, like he was mad at me or something. "Anyway, you could stand to miss a meal. You're getting to look like King Kong Bundy."

Horse laughed. "King Kong Bundy."

"Shut the fuck up," I told him. What did Horse know about King Kong Bundy anyway?

I didn't quite know how to read Shift. He and Horse had been my closest friends for as long as I could remember. But if pressed to name my best friend, I wouldn't have hesitated to say it was Shift. We had never really acknowledged this to each other, but I always figured he felt the same way. Whenever the three of us were together, we laughed a lot, drank a lot, and generally had a good time. But when it was just me and Shift, we talked about stuff while we were drinking and laughing. It wasn't like that with me and Horse.

Shift liked wrestling, and so did I. Horse said he liked wrestling, watched it if it was on, but he didn't know anything about it. He mainly just laughed along with it, as if it was a sit-com. But Shift knew stuff, like I did, and we reminisced a lot over the phone about the likes of Abdullah The Butcher, Dusty Rhodes, and others, challenged each other on trivia, like naming, in order, every single holder of the WWF Intercontinental Championship belt. We made each other cry laughing with the different impersonations of wrestlers we could do. Shift's best was Jake The Snake Roberts and I did a fair Rowdy Roddy Piper. So when Shift compared me to King Kong Bundy, one of the more obese specimens to ever grace the ring, I was truly insulted.

Shift's eyes lit up. Something caught his attention just beyond the terrace. I turned to see George Whitney slide out from the back seat of a silver Mercedes, double parked right beside us on Sainte Catherine Street. Before he closed the door, I caught sight of another guy and two girls in the back seat. One of the girls was dressed in a red tube dress, like she was going to the prom. She was asleep.

Etched on George's perfect face was a permanent smile. He watched his feet as he stepped up onto the sidewalk. Like it was a complicated manoeuvre. Shift called out his name, and George looked up, squinting. Then he saw us. He waved softly and came around the terrace fencing to join us.

As he approached our table he sang out, "Evening, boys," as if we had all been friends forever. "Evening, Gerald," he said to Shift, using his given name like they were business partners or members of the same country club. Shift stood up and the two of them initiated a complicated handshake, one that had to have been rehearsed many times over. George's eyes were glazed and bloodshot. The lids, half-closed, were puffy and heavy looking.

When the handshake was over George grabbed an empty chair nearby and joined us at the table. Settling in, he looked around at us. His faraway eyes focused in on me. His smile grew. "Hey! Rush boy! Yeah, Rush!" He started playing air guitar on the terrace, screwing up his face like he was seriously into it. Then he held his arm straight out at me, fist closed but for his thumb and pinkie. Hang loose. I assumed I was meant to do the same and when I did George met my hand with his, a variant on the classic high-five. "Yeah," he slurred. "*Owner Of A Lonely Heart*. Frigging good song, man."

I refused to correct him this time.

George eyed the open pack of smokes on the table and pulled it toward him with crawling fingers. "Mind if I steal a fine fag?"

Horse giggled. "Fag." I wanted to punch him.

Shift provided a light for George's – our – cigarette. Then Shift put on this real cool voice. "So, what's on the agenda for this evening?"

George dragged on the cigarette, holding it between his thumb and forefinger like a joint. He blew smoke out his nose. "We, my friend, are flying in that fine silver bullet parked out there, over to little Miss Jackie Fournier's abode, whose parents are indisposed and out of town at the moment, where there will be plenty of action and plenty of lovely ladies."

"Sounds mighty fine to me," Shift said in voice that was not his. Real hip cat.

"What about the Crash Test Dummies?" Horse squeaked.

"The *what?*" George asked, squeezing his eyes closed.

"The Crash Test Dummies," Horse repeated. "They're playing down the street tonight."

George shrugged his shoulders, looked to Shift for an explanation. Shift just shrugged, too, as if he didn't know what Horse was talking about. As if he didn't even know Horse at all.

"Come on! You know," Horse said. Before I could stop him he started singing the damned *Superman's Song* song again.

George's face froze. Mouth wide open, eyes shut tight. He started to laugh. Vigorously, cruelly. People at other tables stared at us, he was so loud. I couldn't even look at Horse, I felt so bad for him. I had laughed at him less than an hour before, for the exact same thing, but it wasn't the same. Just as I had felt I didn't have the right to laugh at George for picking his nose, I thought George shouldn't have had the right to laugh at Horse for being Horse.

George couldn't stop, and soon Shift started to laugh, too. The pit of my stomach burned. My ears prickled. George was beyond control, cackling like a sick hyena. He put his hand on Shift's shoulder, feigning a need for leverage. He recovered somewhat. Let out a whoop. "Let's get out of here before I die laughing. Come on." He slapped Shift on the back. "And bring the singing boy with you." The burning rose to my chest.

The table was light, a lot lighter than I expected. I only had to press gently with the ends of my fingers to tip it over. It landed on its side with a dull thud, followed quickly by the crashing of breaking glass. It fell right where I meant it to, right in front of George, the tabletop facing him. The front of his shirt and lap darkened with spilled beer. Shards of broken glass surrounded his feet on the floor. Whatever drugs he had been under the influence of seemed to lose all effect. His face suddenly alert and attentive. Me the centre of his attention.

The bus jerks slightly. The light is green but we only inch along, caught in rubberneck traffic. The dog drama in the McDonald's parking lot has everyone snarled.

The two city workers split up. The one with the lasso pole cuts a wide circle around the dog until he's on the side of the parking lot closest to the street. The dog is between the two of them now. The other guy crouches about fifteen feet away from the dog and slaps the ground with one of his big gloves.

The dog pricks up his ears, still chewing. He cocks his head, studying the gloved city worker. The lasso guy creeps forward a bit, closing the distance between himself and the dog.

"Looks like they're going to rope him in," Horse observes.

A college-aged kid standing in the aisle leans in between Horse and I and the seat behind us. His backpack slides off his arm and thuds against shoulder. "Go doggy! Run, baby, run!" The bus murmurs with laughter. Others start urging the dog to run away, too.

Horse slides his window open. The cold air flows in. Horse puts two fingers to his lips and gives a loud whistle. The dog perks up in our direction. The guy with the lasso looks back at the road, too. Then he moves forward. The dog appears stunned.

The bus is raucous. A chant starts up. "Run! Run! Run! Run!" Horse has one arm out the window, bangs the bus exterior in time with the chant's beat. I find myself joining in. Car horns blast out on the street. The two city workers look bewildered. The dog takes a tentative step away from his garbage bag. The lasso guy lunges at him.

Shift and Horse shot up from their chairs like they'd been electrocuted. George remained seated, looking wet and offended, staring at me. Sodden cigarette dangling from his lips.

Shift tore at his hair, an expression of both anger and fear on his face. "What you do that for? What you do that for?" he screamed. Over and over. I didn't answer him. Couldn't put the answer into words. I only stared back at George. All around us the sounds of chair legs sliding against the floor, the other customers shuffling about and standing up in the confusion.

Beyond George's face I saw two large men emerge from the interior of the bar and step out onto the terrace. The man in the lead was tall and muscular. Solid everywhere except for a waggling belly that hung over his waist, tucked inside a tight purple t-shirt. He marched toward us with a slight limp. The second man was a lot shorter than the first guy, but wider. He wore a Detroit Tigers baseball cap, which he turned backwards on his head as he crossed onto the terrace. Shift stopped yelling at me, and I heard him whisper, "Oh, shit. The bouncers."

Us bus commuters erupt with a cheer as the lasso pole-wielding city worker misses his thrust. Ends up down on the parking lot pavement on all fours. The dog steps away from him, kind of sideways, kind of backwards. Reminds me of a show horse move. The guy with the gloves assumes a defensive stance, like a football player readying to make a tackle. He matches the dog step for step as they move together laterally.

Horse stands up and I can't see. "Get down," I say. But he does more than that. He shuffles on past me and goes into the aisle. He pushes and sidesteps his way toward the front of the bus. "Horse!" I call. But he doesn't look back. I lose sight of him in the crowd. I slide over to his vacated side of our seat and place my forehead against the window. Horse emerge from the bus, squints in the sun. He lopes across the street, between the cars trapped in the traffic jam, and into the McDonald's parking lot. The two city workers note his arrival, but promptly return their attention to the dog. Horse puts two fingers to his lips again.

And we got bounced. All of us.

The fact that Shift had committed no offence deserving of a pummelling meant nothing, and he was punched in the stomach, elbowed in the back, and kicked in the ass. The fact that Horse was a weakling of body and mind and that a beating would most likely scar him for life meant nothing, and he was tripped up by a sideswiping kick, whereupon his stomach and chest were repeatedly stepped on. The fact that George was a business student with lots of family money meant nothing, and he was grabbed from behind, placed in a full-Nelson, slapped in the face, and kneed in the groin.

And the fact that I was just a regular guy with a shish taouk-induced eating disorder, simply trying to stick up for myself and the integrity of my relationship with my friends meant nothing, and I was punched in the nose, head-butted, and kicked in the back of both knees. And as I lay on the sidewalk outside the bar, the blood and the snot dripping and mixing together on the pavement, I smiled painfully, knowing for just that moment, George Whitney had been my equal.

Horse whistles loud and wouldn't you know it, the dog trots right over to him. Nudges Horse's hand with his nose. The other bus riders are rapturous. The college kid shrieks, "Yes! Yes!" Cheers explode from all over. Horns sound anew outside. I just stare in amazement. Horse pats the dogs head, scratches behind his ear. The city workers both smile. Begin to approach. Horse crouches down in front of the dog and rubs its chest. The dog is wagging away with that backwards tail of his. Panting happily. Steamily. Horse reaches around the dog's neck and unfastens the checkered scarf. Stands up again. Then, animal-like, he pitches his face toward the dog's, roars at him. Waves his hands fiendishly. The dog is off, top speed, out of the parking lot, across an adjacent street. He disappears behind a gas station on the corner.

Horse has his hands on his hips, the steam billowing from his mouth, facing the direction of the dog's escape. The city workers are still, look on in disbelief. A hush comes over the bus. Silence. I am the first to applaud. Slowly at first, but I clap faster and the other riders follow my cue. It's a fucking standing ovation. At least from those without seats. Horse turns toward us, he hears it. He's waves the scarf hesitantly. But he's smiling. I've never seen him so happy. So accomplished.

The college kid mutters, "No." Outside, the lasso guy takes a few steps in Horse's direction. Horse turns his head, sees him coming. The worker points at Horse with the business end of his pole. Horse takes a step back. He turns to the bus again. Our eyes meet. He looks like a terrified child.

The Barenaked Ladies were already on stage by the time Horse and I turned up at the concert. Indeed, they were not a chick band, as Shift had mused, if only jokingly. I had never seen anybody so portly fronting a band. Thick-framed glasses and chunky sideburns, too. I felt like there was some hope for the world. Even if their music was cheesy. Horse loved it, though. Bought their tape at the end of their set. He still talks about it now, owning their tape before *If I Had $1000000* ever played on the radio. As if he discovered them.

We all need something special to hang on to.

Shift did not attend the show with us. He crawled into the back seat of that silver bullet of a Mercedes along with his buddy George and the rest of the Commerce and Management posse. I presume he got laid multiple times at the big party. I never got to hear about it. They held the door open for Horse, but he waved them off with a polite refusal.

And you should have seen him sing along with the Crash Test Dummies when they finally took the stage.

I get up from my seat and work my way to the front of the bus. Convince the reluctant driver to let me out. The two city workers are chewing Horse out. The bus is chanting "Leave him alone! Leave him alone!" Traffic begins to crawl a little faster and I cut and duck across the street. The chanting grows progressively quieter as the bus pulls away. I step over a little island of concrete and walk into the parking lot. See if can lend some support.

HOT DOGS ON EVERYTHING

High school students and anybody who was drunk made up the majority of Julio's clientele. He put chopped up hot dog wieners on everything – pizzas, souvlaki, subs, hamburger steak, fish and chips. A popular menu item, particularly after midnight, was the Cannibal Dog: a jumbo hot dog garnished with mustard, ketchup, coleslaw, and chopped up hot dog wieners.

When Julio dreamed up the idea, Veronica said it would fail for sure. Veronica had a BA in Economics. Julio liked to joke that his wife could argue convincingly for either side of the Gold Standard vs. Silver Standard debate, but the register was somehow always short at least two bucks every night at closing. This kind of teasing made the crease come out on Veronica's chin as she tried to suppress her smile. She'd look down at her shoes and bite her thumbnail, a few curly strands of hair hanging tantalizingly in front of her forehead. "Just chop your wieners, big man. Big genius."

Veronica wore short skirts behind the cash register. When things got slow mid-afternoons, a slip of one of Julio's dishpan hands up amidst her curves, crooks, dips and hooks made up for the long hours, the tired nights. Hot dogs on everything was going to put their daughter, Hillary, through college.

Seth Kordich ran the Smiling Grub Stop down the road. Hot dogs on everything was killing his business. Over swigs from his vodka bottle, Seth considered cutting his milkshake prices in half, toyed briefly with the idea of ground beef and fried onions on everything, but finally settled on saving his restaurant with the business end of a baseball bat.

Seth polio-limped into Julio and Veronica's place slurring and screaming, brandishing his bat. He smashed the salt and pepper shakers, sugar distributors and ketchup bottles on the tables, ignoring terrified customers rushing past him out the door. Veronica grabbed the fire extinguisher behind the counter and ran at Seth, foam spraying. Julio followed close behind with his hot dog cleaver. Seth took a wild swing at the pair and connected with the side of Veronica's skull. Julio hacked him down where he stood.

Veronica forgot the finer points of Keynes and Galbraith but, in time, thanks to Hillary's diligence and patience, re-learned the workings of the cash register. Most nights she balanced, but there was precious little to count as even hot dogs on everything could not prevail against the stain of disrepute that hovered over the restaurant. Though local sentiment was practically unanimous in considering Julio's actions justified, nobody wanted to eat at what the teenagers had taken to calling "Death Diner."

Five years later, Hillary took out her first in a series of student loans and commenced undergraduate studies in Sociology at a college three hours away by bus. Near the end of her first semester she happened upon a misplaced wallet between desks in one of the larger lecture halls. Inside she found ninety dollars. She treated herself and her roommates to pizza, beer and cigarettes and felt easy and free for a few days, anyway.

ALL THE WAY TO THE DUMP

I was this close to dumping my boyfriend yesterday.

He's good-looking and everything. Clean, too. He doesn't have any body hair except for his armpits, pubes, and this little patch on the small of his back that isn't really all that noticeable.

Kenny is a rock star in the making, but he hasn't played a gig in nearly a year. He's fucking lazy and the other guys in Coagulated are dense and directionless; together they are a finely tuned apathy machine.

What's sad is that Kenny actually has potential. During his good periods, when he's writing, playing, and drinking a ton, he's sexy as all hell. Other girls are crazy about him. At his shows they crowd the slim space between the edge of the stage and the edge of the mosh pit, writhe around with their arms outstretched and beg Kenny to touch them. Once one gets touched the others swarm her and go into this big pseudo lesbo ritual, lick the spot. After the shows they try and rush the room backstage, pleading to get in. Some say it's an act, the worshipping. But it's not. I know. I used to be one of those girls.

A critic from this local weekly did a piece on Kenny a couple years ago, described him as "a young, effeminate Joey Ramone." She got it partially right. Kenny's got these killer blue eyes that he encircles with thick black makeup. He usually wears green or black lipstick. He's pierced all over; ears, right eyebrow, bottom lip, right

nipple, and, especially right before a show, he's into bigger, temporary patterns. Once, I slipped forty-six sterilized extra large safety
pins into the skin of his back, forming a pretty damned symmetrical
pentagram for an amateur. That night, after the show, I removed
them for him slow and easy in our bed, me kneeling behind him and
him reaching back with those delicate and dexterous guitar-player
fingers of his and I still get revved up just thinking about that time,
that Kenny.

But his periods of malaise are depressing and debilitating, and go
on too long. I finally got fed up with his latest funk, forced him into
an agreement. He might be a rock star but I've got my shit, too. I do
comics and had some good stuff going until I let it slide to support
us both by waitressing in a crappy 24-hour deli that smelled like
mustard and Ajax, where I had the displeasure of serving drunk and
obnoxious college boys at 4 AM, their appetites for smoked meat and
fries fuelled by the booze in their bellies that they *had* to know would
be riding back up their throats and out their gaping puke mouths by
the end of the night.

Worse was Nikko, the Grecian Formula-tinted owner who never
seemed to go home. He put his chapped hands on me way too often,
his fingers dry like breadsticks. All suave, he played up my fatigue,
offered massages. I'd squirm out of his clutches the best I could. One
night, when it was real slow in the place, I was leaning on the counter, reading the *Allo Police*. Nikko snuck up from behind and put his
hand up the back of my skirt. When I recoiled he said he had been
reaching for an errant thread and misjudged his aim, apologized.
Then in the next breath hissed, "I like those little underwears,
though."

"Hey, I know a great place for thongs," I replied, detached and
sarcastic at the same time. "I'll be sure to give your wife the address

next time she comes by." Nikko backed off a bit, but a week later the chase was on again. He was total scum.

I was wasting my time, giving up nearly thirty hours a week so Kenny and I could keep our apartment while he sat at home, presumably getting his music career back on track, when all he was doing was sleeping, eating bowl after bowl of Cap'n Crunch, and watching his Star Trek tapes. I told him if he wasn't doing anything musically, he might as well get a job, pay the rent for both of us, let me have a turn at being supported for once, get back to my comics. It might even be good for him, I told him, to get out there and work. Clear out his head. Get him back to where he needed to be, mentally.

Kenny surprised me and agreed. Within a week he landed a job at Purolator to load and unload freight in their warehouse. He went through the whole orientation process, the physical, the training, the fitting for his uniforms. I did my last shift at the deli the night before Kenny's first day. Instead of two weeks notice I gave Nikko two swift boots to the groin. He called me a dirty bitch and I was free.

I got home at about seven-thirty and Kenny was still in bed. His shift was supposed to start at six. He smelled like beer and farts and I slapped him in the head five or six times, punched him in the stomach, I was crying, and even with all that he barely woke up. Didn't until noon. I forced him to call Purolator. He said it was hopeless and I knew it was, too, but all the same I wanted him to try. They said he could forget about the job and they expected the uniforms back by the end of the week.

I couldn't dump him. I wanted to so badly but I was terrified he'd go and get busy again. Get sexy again. It wouldn't take him long to find somebody else to take him in, one of his little groupies with a counter job at Wal-Mart or Burger King. I paid a visit to Employment Canada.

Because I'd quit the deli, Sylvain, my friendly-but-bored job rep informed me, the only way I could get any amount of EI was if I entered some kind of a training program. I said sure. Figured I could sleep through whatever they put me in during the day, work on my comics at night, and keep up with the rent until Kenny got some semblance of his act together and found another job.

"What kind of work are you interested in?" Sylvain asked, stifling a yawn.

"Honestly, I can't decide. What do you suggest?" Like I cared.

"What about Personal Care Work? It's the wave of the future," he mumbled, so unenthused. He showed me a pamphlet from his desk. The cover said *PCW: The Wave of the Future*. Sylvain read from the pamphlet, he might have been reading Kraft Dinner ingredients he was so bored, stuff about aging populations, rising demand for home care, bathing, feeding, and a bunch of things I really couldn't care about. I said sure, sign me up, and I started my classes the next week.

There was no way to sleep through this program. It was all hands-on. "Point your fingers back at your own eyes after you hook your arms under the shoulders," Brenda, our rather rotund instructor barked as I struggled with the stupid androgynous geriatric mannequin. It was purple and so un-lifelike. So dead. "Lift with your legs, not your back!" I couldn't wait for the cigarette breaks.

The Friday after the first week of classes I was beat. I just wanted to crawl under the blankets, grab a twelve-hour sleep session, do some recovering. But when I got home Kenny was sprawled across the bed with his jeans still on, stinking again, a drool spot on the sheet beneath his face. I shook him a little, told him to hit the couch. No response. I shook him again, clapped my hands next to his ear. He wouldn't wake up, just mumbled disjointed nonsense about Geddy Lee and Hamburger Helper. I tried pulling him off the bed by his arms, but he was a dead weight. I then realized I was approaching the problem all wrong. I put my newly-acquired skills to work.

I went off to retrieve our computer chair and wheeled it over near the bed, placed its back to the wall to keep it steady. I got into bed beside Kenny, on my knees, and eased him up into a sitting position. I hooked my arms at the elbows under his armpits and lifted with a puff and a pant. My deadbeat boyfriend was considerably heavier than the purple dummy at class, and his limbs flopped around in unpredictable ways. I managed to get him into the chair, though, and he stayed all peaceful, all snores. I wheeled him down the hall to the kitchen and left him facing the window where the sun comes in blazing every morning.

I woke the next morning in a panic, heart thumping. I was sure I was late for class. By the time I figured out it was Saturday, there was no getting back to sleep. I craved coffee. In the kitchen I found Kenny still in the computer chair, still facing the window. I allowed myself to imagine for a second he was dead. I got all creeped out, two lines of chill crawled up the sides of my neck and I shuddered. I stood motionless and held my breath, listening for his breath and staring at the top of the back of his head, his hair scrunched and splayed where it rested against the chair. He let out a little gurgle of a snore. I spun the chair around to face me. "Rise and shine, lazy-ass!"

Kenny's head slumped forward and bounced back to its original position. "Tired," he mumbled.

"Let's go. Get up. This place is a bloody mess."

"Can't." Kenny crossed one leg over the other, crossed his arms and smacked his lips, fell deeper into sleep. Pathetic son of a bitch, I thought. He looked peaceful, like an unshaven baby, sitting there asleep in the chair. He could have been lying in a prince's bed, silk sheets and loose-fitting pyjamas. He probably didn't even know such a thing as comfortable pyjamas existed and, despite it, could sleep forever in a dirty pair of jeans and wake up just before dying and smile, content with the life he'd slept. In that moment, two things occurred to me: one, how I wished so very much I had the kind of boyfriend who made me coffee in the morning, because coffee always tastes so much better when somebody else makes it, and, two, that my boyfriend was so totally disposable. Literally.

I slipped my right arm between Kenny's back and the chair and had him on his feet within seconds, my hands clasped together against his chest, the bends of my arms hooked under his armpits. He felt light. I dragged him backwards through the kitchen door, him snoring away, and down the hall. I leaned my back hard against the door of our apartment, rested Kenny against my body, and freed one of my hands to feel blindly for the lock and the handle. I hauled Kenny out into the communal hall, hoping none of the other tenants were coming or going, hoping nobody would see me trying to stuff my boyfriend down the garbage chute.

The realization that he'd probably sleep all the way to the dump made me laugh out loud.

Kenny stiffened and turned, his eyes wide and confused. "Why am I out here? What are we doing?"

"Having tea with the Queen, what does it look like we're doing?"

"It looks like we're in the hallway and you're in your underwear." His reply was so genuine I had to punch him in the chest. "Fuck," he coughed. "That hurt. Let's go back in. I got a new song I need to play you. You have to promise not to laugh, it's about us."

He's a sexy man, my Kenny.

BESTER McNALLY'S FOWL TALE

Bester McNally worked the day shift at the Sticky Fingers Rotisserie, had for 43 years, was five shifts away from retirement.

Bester was the chicken master at Sticky Fingers, the highest-ranking position attainable short of day or night manager. Like a beer company's brewmaster, or a dough expert at a pizzeria, Bester was responsible for the quality and production of the restaurant's show-case product: its barbecue chicken. It was Bester who oversaw the process of removing just the right number of chickens from the freezer for thawing at exactly the right time. It was Bester who maintained the roasting ovens, getting them warmed up in the morning, ensuring the chickens would be ready in time for the lunch rush, and making small repairs to the one hundred individual spits whenever necessary. So many years of experience made doing his job a routine as natural and automatic for Bester as getting dressed in the morning, and with one pair of jeans, three white T-shirts, a baseball cap, and a hairnet to his name, it was a simple routine. Over the course of 43 years at Sticky Fingers, Bester had run deliveries, done spot duty on overnight maintenance and cleaning, worked the cash register, painted the place four times, and even filled in now and then for waitresses too crampy or hungover to come in for their shifts. At 62 years of age, Bester had four teeth left in his mouth, bowels that ran like a faucet, a purple, irregularly-shaped spot on the side of his nose, and an intimate knowledge of the operations of a barbecue chicken restaurant that even the managers couldn't approach in its detail or scope.

But Bester had no desire for command, for the opulence of management with its blue-sweater uniforms, a pencil behind the ear, and access to the back-office desk that had seen its share of propped-up-feet over the years. Bester liked being chicken master and strove no higher, especially now so close to retirement. For the Sticky Fingers Rotisserie management team, this was a blessing that had lasted 43 years. There wasn't a better chicken master in town; quality and production were never in doubt with Bester on the job. They laughed a little at him behind closed doors – about the care and attention he put into his work, above and beyond what was required for the $9.38 an hour they paid him. They often sighed, unlocking the front door in the morning to find Bester had slept in the restaurant again, keeping an eye on some tricky oven element or some clogged oil vat, and said to themselves, "Look at him. This is all he has." And they counted their lucky stars for having *him*.

But Bester McNally had a secret. He could have taken over the whole restaurant long ago, been a manager for years. But he stayed on as chicken master because he had a gift. Bester McNally could talk to the dead, and his favourite conversation partners were dead chickens.

Bester started talking to dead chickens as a boy, in his grandmother's drafty kitchen, heated by an oil stove. His grandmother wore boots in the house in winter, was able to hoist forty-pound sacks of potatoes over her shoulder, and had a purple, irregularly-shaped spot on the side of her nose. She spread table salt on her icy balcony to prevent accidents.

Chicken was his grandmother's best meal. She was a walking chicken recipe book. Broiled Devilled Chicken. Marinated Broilers. Chicken Marseillaise. Hunter's Chicken. Chicken Fritters. Supreme

Chicken. Fried Hen. Skewered Chicken Livers. Auntie Diane's Fried Chicken. Chicken Burgers. And all of it deboned and cut up into bite-sized morsels for Bester; his grandmother had a mortal fear of choking accidents.

She never stopped to eat herself – once Bester was served his grandmother hooked a cigarette in the corner of her mouth and went to work on his second and third helpings. One evening, hunched over the pots and pans on the stove, she turned her head and watched him take a bite of Chicken Paprika. "Oh, you're so good," she cried, cigarette bobbing with every syllable. "The little chickens are so happy, they're dancing for joy!" Bester giggled and stuffed five bites of Chicken Paprika in his mouth. His grandmother inhaled a deep, audible gasp that sounded like dull fingernails scratching on a chalkboard. "Spit that out! You're going to choke!" Bester complied, allowed the spicy chicken to lop out of his mouth onto the plate. "Now eat it nice and slow," his grandmother said, serenity returning to her voice. "The chickens want you to *enjoy* it."

In his mind, young Bester saw five chickens on a patch of dusty ground, smiles on their beaks, holding each other's wings, dancing in a circle. High in the sky the sun shone bright and warm, a cool breeze in the air. One of the chickens said, "Eat *me* next, Bester!" Another chimed in, "No, me! Eat me! I'm best served fried!" Bester laughed and told them not to worry, he'd be sure to eat all of them, every one.

In time, Bester learned that cheeseburgers made cows throw a party. Veal cutlets had calves cooing and tittering. Hot dogs caused pigs to sing songs of happiness and kiss each other. But the chickens were the best. When his grandmother cooked chicken they gathered at his feet, tickling his toes with their pecking beaks, clucking up waves and waves of suggestions. "A little honey sure does a lot for a basket of fried chicken!" "Every try a chicken quesadilla? You'll like it!" They never stopped talking, and, after his grandmother passed on, the spot on her nose spreading out and colonizing a good portion of her right cheek by the end, they were all he had to talk to.

Gravitating to a chicken-related line of work was a necessity both financial and social. For 43 years Bester cooked three hundred chickens or more every day. The dead chickens took advantage of their numbers and organized hoedowns, picnics, and softball games to celebrate the fact that people were eating them. Bester took part in the activities, befriending generations of dead chickens along the way.

Bester felt fortunate to have had so many years in the company of dead chickens, could never quite get over the idea that he was actually being paid for it. But it was coming to an end, and he was looking forward to the rest. He'd been imagining his life after the Sticky Fingers Rotisserie. He figured he could get by on three chickens a week; leftovers never really bothered him.

Five shifts to go, but first he was going on a little day trip. All of the Sticky Fingers employees and even some of the regular customers chipped in and bought Bester a retirement gift: a tour of a chicken farm, something he'd never done. They even paid for a taxicab rather than send him off on an hour-long bus ride to the country.

The cab picked him up at the Sticky Fingers. He crawled into the back seat, aided by one of the waitresses, chewing gum snapping in his ear. The other employees, gathered in the parking lot, waved to him as the cab pulled out. When the taxi turned onto the highway Bester felt a little tingling in his ears and a sudden onset of heartburn, not an unexpected sensation: he'd eaten at the Sticky Fingers yet again. He closed his eyes in the backseat, knowing a little nap would have him feeling chipper by the time he got to the farm.

The cabby shook him from his sleep. "Hey Gramps. You're here. And by the way, you're friends didn't pony up for a tip."

Bester handed the man a crumpled five-dollar bill and pulled himself from the car. He barely had time to shut the door before the cab sped off, heading back to civilization.

Bester took a moment to absorb it all. The farm was just as he'd imagined it. The taxi had driven him up a winding dirt road and left him in front of a white-painted farmhouse with red trim, blacktop roof, and a brick chimney, smoke softly curling from the stack. A wide cornfield lay to his left, forest of trees to his right. Big red barn standing next to a grain silo in a patch of land adjacent to the corn. A farmer in a floppy straw hat, green overalls, and thick boots, blowing his nose into a handkerchief, stood on the farmhouse porch.

"Welcome to the Cross Winds," the farmer said, folding his handkerchief, stuffing it into his back pocket. He descended the four short steps from the balcony to the road and extended his hand. "Name's Ken. Ken Norton, like the boxer, 'cepting he was quite a shade darker than myself." Farmer Ken laughed at his own joke, coughed, took out his handkerchief again.

"I'm Bester McNally. I've been chicken master at Sticky Fingers Rotisserie almost, well, almost all my life. Sure am looking forward to seeing your operation here. Are the other people on the tour here yet?"

"Other people?" Ken Norton the farmer cried. "There's no other people. Just you, Mr. Bester."

Bester felt happy to know his friends had gone out and got him a real special tour. "So when can we start?"

"Well, right away, just as soon as we get some formalities out of the way. Come on over to the barn and we can get started, get you cleaned up a little."

The barn was musty. Chicken coops, stacked four high, stretched in rows from one end to the other. A narrow passage bisected the rows. The hum of clucking inside was so thick it sounded to Bester like the motor of an air conditioner gone awry.

Farmer Ken got down on one knee in front of Bester, took hold of his ankle. Bester pulled back instinctively. "Now, now," Farmer Ken said. "Just hold still, this'll only take a second." He wrapped something that felt like a bracelet around Bester's ankle.

"What the hell is that?" Bester asked, flapping at what looked like a yellow price tag hanging from his ankle off a thin metal wire.

"Well, gotta be able to identify you. 'Stinguish you from the rest."

Bester had no time to ask further when Farmer Ken wrapped his fingers around his jaw, forcing his mouth open. With his other hand he guided Bester's head back. Bester's mouth was suddenly filled with pellets that felt like M&Ms but tasted like aspirins.

"Whhhhhh."

"Got to get you filled up with antibiotics, there. Want you to be healthy, you know." Farmer Ken cupped his palm over Bester's mouth and held it there until he swallowed all the antibiotics.

Gagging, Bester managed to blurt out: "You're crazy! I want to go home. I want to go back to the Sticky Fingers. Now!"

"No, no, no," Farmer Ken said, "the whole thing's been set up, all paid for. You can't leave *now*."

Bester sat down on the dusty floor of the barn, exhausted. He heard clicking and looked up to see Ken shaking a spray paint can, walking toward him. Ken rolled Bester's right shirtsleeve up and painted his entire arm yellow. "For quick ID," the farmer said, answering Bester's unasked question.

Bester felt terrible. Sick to his stomach and dizzy in his head. He just wanted to sleep.

"One more step and then I'll put you up so you can rest," Farmer Ken said, hoisting Bester to his feet. He was led down the rows of coops, the chickens throwing themselves at the wire mesh as he passed. "They're a little antsy today," Ken said, chuckling. "But they get like that with newcomers."

At the end of the barn Farmer Ken sat Bester down on an over-turned wooden crate. Bester rested his chin in his hands. Ken walked over to some kind of a machine, a metal box with a cylinder connected to its side. Ken flicked a switch and the cylinder began spinning, slowly at first but soon so fast it was a blur. Farmer Ken hooked his arms under Bester's armpits and dragged him over to the machine. "Believe me," the farmer said, "this is going to hurt me a lot more than it's going to hurt you. But it's for the best – I don't want you harming anybody – nobody wants to buy chickens all pecked up." Ken angled Bester's face toward the spinning cylinder. He felt a great heat emanating from it. He had no strength to resist and blacked out in the very instant the circular saw dug into the flesh, cartilage, and bone of his nose.

CASUAL SEX
BOOKENDED BY TWO GRATUITOUS
HOT DOG PIZZA SCENES

I'm seventeen and I'm bored and my Dad is walking in the door after work. He's carrying a pizza. My mother has a chicken going in the oven, but she isn't mad because, like all of us, she's so genuinely surprised.

My Dad acts the big hero, fake magnanimous shit, as if he does generous stuff all the time. He places the pizza box on the dining room table and points at it with his whole hand like it's Bob Barker's next item up for bid. We put up with it – it's pizza, after all. I even catch my sister smiling for a second. My Dad flips the box open, all proud. "Who's first?"

The pizza is covered with round, pink slices of hot dog wieners. Green peppers and mushrooms are also evident, along with melted cheese and red tomato sauce, but the wieners give the pizza a ghastly appearance. I can't help but think of severed fingertips.

"That's sick," my sister sneers.

"What the hell were you thinking?" asks my Mom, deridingly.

I turn away. In the vestibule, I step into my running shoes and pull my red polar fleece over my head. I back out the front door as the insults start to really fly.

Outside it's cool and dark. A pleasant wave of anticipation penetrates my shoulders, neck and head as I finger the change in my pocket and contemplate the depanneur down on the main road that sells single cigarettes. Halfway there I cross paths with one of the Lavoie twins, jogging. She's wearing a green K-Way and black spandex pants. She stops and says hi. She has dark, super short hair, small brown eyes and thick, pale lips. Her skin is murky white and her pulse throbs in the crevice where her neck meets her collarbone. The Lavoies went to my high school but I haven't seen either of them since we started going to different Cégeps. Both sisters jog regularly and I guess right when I say "Hi Caroline."

We talk, walking, about mutual friends at our respective schools, the complications of getting downtown on a daily basis from where we live, the impending Christmas break. Caroline pauses at a lamppost, to stretch. She steadies herself against it with one hand and reaches behind herself with the other to grab the heel of her shoe, bending one of her thin legs at the knee. Her supporting leg curves backwards slightly – she's limber as all shit. She switches legs and reports she's dying for a drink of water, gestures to her house a few doors up the street. That I'm invited to join her is obvious.

Inside, Caroline pulls off her K-Way and throws it on the floor of the vestibule closet, revealing a neat black T-shirt with extra-short sleeves, tight around her small breasts. I follow her to the kitchen where, standing in front of the open refrigerator, she downs half the contents of a water bottle. The silence feels awkward to me, and I inquire about her sister. "Juliette has lacrosse practice Wednesdays. My Mom's gone to pick her up. Come upstairs."

In her room, Caroline produces a joint flattened between the pages of a *Norton Anthology of English Literature, Volume 1*. She opens a window and lights up, beckons me over. We lean out the window together, our elbows brushing gently against each other, pass the joint back and forth. It's a little harsh, but I'm not about to complain.

I stare at Caroline's family's back yard, the house behind their hedge, the house behind that one. The row of streetlamps on the adjacent road with their slightly distorted orange glow. Caroline flicks the smoked joint away with a snap of her middle finger and thumb. I watch the red ember dive bomb to the ground.

I pull my head inside and feel my buzz a little heavier in the room air. Caroline closes the window and draws the shade. She places her wrists on my shoulders, her fingers lightly grazing my back. She stares right into my eyes and for a second I think she's going to start slow-dancing with me. Automatically, I put my hands on her hips, my palms and fingers straight, like a shy kid in Grade 4. She goes up on her toes and kisses me, hard, her lips working my mouth open. Her tongue entangles itself with mine, then darts about, exploring other parts of my mouth. She grips the back of my neck with one hand and lowers the other to the small of my back, pulls me hard against herself and commences to grind.

I work her shirt up past her breasts, snug in a grey sports bra that flips up easily enough. She raises her arms and I slip everything over her head, my palms glancing over her armpits, slightly picky with short stubble and chalky with antiperspirant residue. I feel her shiver against me and her kissing intensifies, our teeth clinking. Her breasts are soft, the flesh spongy and yielding. They fit entirely inside the grip of each of my hands. Caroline exhales hard out her nose, her breath cool on my wet top lip, reaches under my shirt and twist-squeezes one of my nipples. I sigh and laugh at the same time.

In her bed, on top of her unmade blankets and sheets, I receive a quick introduction to the box of condoms in her bedside table drawer. I get inside her easily and finish quick, embarrassingly quick, but good nonetheless.

Free of me, Caroline, businesslike, sits up and turns around, faces the other way. She grabs a pillow and places it behind herself, lays her head on it. She raises both legs and rests her feet on her bed's headboard, toes turned in to face each other. She goes to work on herself with both hands. Soon she's moaning, steady at first, then quickening. She sounds like she's asking the same question over and over again in some ancient, guttural language. I watch, unsure of my role in it all. Her legs begin to buck, matching time with her breathing. I reach out for one of her breasts, gently take hold of it. My hand is pushed away, firmly.

The thought occurs to me to leave the room, but I don't sense I'm completely unwelcome. Caroline's moaning deepens. The rhythm of her hands accelerates. Her hips rise from the bed and her back arches as she comes, goose bumps dotting her upper arms and thighs. She collapses to the bed with a sigh and a smile.

Then she's up, crouched over a record collection lined up on the floor against a wall, her vertebrae bumpy down her sinewy back, flipping through albums. The room is painted pink and a cheesy floral wallpaper border is plastered around the four walls beneath the ceiling. Juliette's bed is identical to Caroline's but made, a few books scattered at the foot of it.

Caroline slips a record from its jacket and places it on her player. She holds the needle delicately between her thumb and forefinger, drops it gently near the beginning of the record. A little crackle and then *Mandinka* by Sinead O'Connor starts up. With arms outstretched, Caroline invites me to dance.

I can't dance and I try to make light of it by putting on some really bad moves on purpose, show that I'm joking around. She laughs, almost charitably, then, like before, becomes engrossed in herself. Her head shimmies, athletic legs spring left and right, doing a stationary slalom, arms pumping. I tell myself I could love this girl. She mouths all the lyrics, skinny naked body bopping, her short hair motionless atop all the commotion. I sit back down on the bed halfway through the song and Caroline keeps dancing, the record skipping once near the end. She bangs the floor with one foot and the music rights itself.

When the song is over she replaces the needle and throws her T-shirt back on, not bothering with the bra. I follow her lead and start to dress. "That was a hell of a lot of fun," she surprises me by saying. I feel relieved, accepted. She glances at a Strawberry Shortcake alarm clock. "You better get out of here. I'll show you down."

I buy two single cigarettes and a Coke at the depanneur and walk home slowly, the inside of my mouth tasting steadily ranker and sweeter. When I get in, everybody is sleeping and I'm starving. I find the pizza in the fridge, still in its grease-stained box, half eaten, all the hot dog chunks picked off, crusting along the sides of the box. I eat three slices cold and go to bed with my jeans on.

DYSFUNCTION JUNCTION

HIGH SCORE

Bob is spent.

But his full attention is still required. Somehow, entering his name is always more unnerving than the actual game play. It's the 30 second timer. It's the way the cursor is limited to only left-to-right or right-to-left movements. He can't go up or down. It's such a long way from the *B* to the *O*. And then all the way back to *B* again. It's the way, even after all three letters of his name have been inputted, he must still enter *END*. Before the time runs out. He doesn't know what would happen if he didn't enter *END*. He has never dared try.

His name is in. He exhales mightily. He loves that his name is short enough to fit. It's more authentically him. No need for un-fortunately impersonal initials or, worse, an indecipherable abbre-viation. And, he does not understand why anyone would waste their achievement on a childish entry like ASS or SEX. Or FUK.

There, for everyone to see, even when he isn't there, in pixels clear as day, the high score on the Donkey Kong Junior machine at the arcade at the mall belongs to BOB.

SOME TROUBLE WITH A TOW TRUCK DRIVER

"Flash that guy!" Leandra shrieks. She's in the front passenger seat of the station wagon. Bob is driving. Danny, their ten-year old son, is in the back seat. Bob isn't listening. "Flash him now! He cut you off!"

Leandra leans hard to the left and reaches across Bob's lap. Her heart is racing. She probes with her fingers for the headlight switch to the left of the steering wheel. Finds it. She flicks the high beams on and off repeatedly, in quick succession. Her head feels like it's filled with sludge that wasn't there before. "Son of a fucking bitch."

She feels the car slow down. Stop. She sits back up. They are stopped for a red light, at least ten cars back of the intersection, taillights glowing red in the darkness. The tow truck that slipped from the right lane into theirs a minute ago is in front of them. "Bastard."

"He didn't exactly cut us off," Bob says.

"Pushover."

"What's going on?" Danny pops his head between Leandra and Bob, leaning over the top of the front seat bench. He spins the cylinder of his toy revolver and snaps it with his palm to stop it. Neil Diamond's *Heartlight* is playing on the radio.

"There's a crazy driver in front of us. That's what's going on." Leandra punches the horn. Holds down on it. Bob pushes her hand away.

Ahead, the tow truck's door swings open. The driver slips out and turns to face them. He's wearing a short sleeved, light blue work shirt, a good portion of the top buttons undone. His pants are a darker shade of blue. Beige work boots. He reaches back into the cab of his truck, retrieves a pair of yellow and black gloves. He pulls them on, slowly, methodically.

"What the hell is he doing?" Leandra asks. Nobody replies.

The tow truck driver reaches back into his cab. This time he produces a chain, as long as his arm. He stands still for a moment, staring them down, the chain dangling like a dead snake from his right hand. He marches toward their car, a little strut in his stride. His face is blank.

"Run him over!" Leandra's head feels like it's on fire now. "Run him over, he's going to kill us!" She grabs the steering wheel with her left hand, rotates it left and right, fruitlessly. "Run him down!"

Bob gently but firmly removes her hand from the steering wheel. She watches him signal left. He creeps forward slightly in that direction. She can't believe he's fucking signalling. He U-turns and joins traffic heading in the opposite direction. Leandra looks back. The tow truck driver is climbing back into his truck. "You should have run that bastard over."

Bob says nothing.

THE BUNS, THE MELBA TOASTS, THE BREADSTICKS

Their favourite restaurant is Le Miracle, a 24-hour deli where everything on the menu goes for half-price between midnight and five in the morning. On the nights they eat out, Danny goes to bed with his clothes on, hungry but happy, knowing he'll be tackling menu item number 48, *Ravioli Colossal*, before the sun comes up.

They are shown to a booth with dark blue vinyl seats. Half the tables in the restaurant are occupied, but Danny notes that he is, as usual, the only kid in the place. It's a point of pride.

Conversation is spare as they look over the menus. Bob's declaration that he might try the rib steak sounds forced; a thinly-veiled attempt to get everyone's mind off of the tow truck driver.

After ordering, a bread basket and glasses of water are delivered to their booth. Danny snatches a bun. He's famished. His father reaches for one, too. Danny butters his bun, but he's also watching Leandra. He can't see her hands beneath the table but he knows she has placed her purse in her lap. Her eyes look all around her but her head doesn't move at all. She's really good at this stuff. With one finger, she drags the breadbasket closer to her. She proceeds to empty it of its contents, one by one, delivering each item to her lap. Danny can't see it, but he knows it's all going into her purse; the buns, the Melba Toasts, the breadsticks. His mother pushes the basket to the center of the table again and all that's left are some crumbs and one single-serving butter container.

A busboy passes the table. Bob calls him back. Points at the empty bread basket. "Another one, please."

PARENTAL DISCRETION ADVISED

The Late Night Movie is on the TV. A drama. Danny is lying in his bed. His parents are sitting up in theirs. The television is centered between the two beds. All the lights in the motel room are out.

Danny isn't allowed to watch the movie. As far as he can gather, this is because the movie features a lot of kissing, a lot of crying, and a lot of shouting. Plus, a snippet of the song *Torn Between Two Lovers* plays before and after each commercial break.

"Turn around!" his mother hisses.

"I'm comfortable on this side."

"Face the other way. You can't watch this. It's not for kids."

"I don't WANT to watch it. I'm just comfortable like this."

"I said turn over!"

"Couldn't I just go read in the bathroom?"

"No. It's late. Now. Turn. Around. Do it."

Danny twists his body to face the other way. Stares at the drawn patio curtains. The colour of Dijon mustard. The beige carpet. His toy gun lying on the ground. The wooden legs of the chair in front of the writing desk. The writing desk, the mirror above it. The television is reflected in the mirror.

He feels guilty and excited at the same time. He sees a woman with red hair. She's wearing a bathrobe. A man with grey hair is kissing her neck. He's wearing a suit and tie. The woman throws her head back with her eyes closed, her mouth open. Danny shifts slightly to lie on his stomach, pressing his erection between himself and the mattress, snug.

"You better not be listening to this!"

Danny pulls the pillow over his head. "Happy?" he yells, muffled.

"Don't get smart."

Danny squashes his face into the mattress. He draws the pillow down harder on top of his head and screams into the sheets.

JUST ONE GAME

Bob's got a pleasant morning coffee buzz and a station wagon full of telephone books. The brand new edition for 1983/84. A list of addresses on the passenger seat beside him. It's the third day of what the guy who hired him said would be five days of work. A week, tops. Either way, Bob should make enough to get the motel manager off his back and keep them from being tossed out on the street. And, with summer waning and the beginning of a new school year only a few weeks away, a good string of stints as a substitute could get them out of the motel and back into an apartment. Bob hopes for luck and lots of sick teachers.

But Bob received more than just the day's allotment of phone books this morning at the depot: he also got paid for his first two days on the job. Cash. Now he's on his way to play just one game of Donkey Kong Junior before starting. He figures he can make up the time by not stopping for lunch. He realizes it wouldn't bee too difficult to find a Donkey Kong Junior machine somewhere in the vicinity of his delivery area, but he wants to see his name at the top of the high score list again as much as he wants to play. So it's back to the mall down the street from the motel.

Bob is abundantly pleased with his accomplishment. He carries his pride around like a tin of snuff, dipping into it when he remembers he's got it. Or when he needs it. It props him up, gives him a temporary glow. But his pride is unrequited – he can't share it. To let others know about his Donkey Kong Junior prowess would be akin to reaching into his mouth and pulling out that wet, soppy clump of chewing tobacco and offering to share.

He wishes he could tell Leandra about it. Hear a wife's compliments. Some awe for a gifted husband. He cringes to imagine her reaction should she ever find out about the time and, more importantly, the money he's been spending on arcade games.

Even more, he wishes Danny knew. Sons are supposed to be proud of their fathers, he laments. Some dads know their way around a workbench. Some dads can throw a football 50 yards. This dad can drop fruit on Snapjaws practically at will and climb vines like nobody's business.

Bob grips the steering wheel tighter. The mall is in sight. Just one game, he tells himself. Just one game, and back to work. Just one game. Then he'll feel better.

SO SUMPTUOUS AND LUSCIOUS

Danny is hungry. His mother tells him they are going to eat a little later. He waits until she goes into the shower.

Danny turns up the volume on the television. Rhino's thunderous raging against Spider-Man combines with the drone of the fan and running water from the bathroom. He hopes it's enough noise to mask his foraging. He inspects the drawers of the tables on either side of the big bed but only finds stationery and a Gideon Bible. Danny lies down on the scratchy wall-to-wall carpeting beside his mother's side of the bed. Hunkered there, slumped and flabby, burgundy and forbidding, is Leandra's purse.

Danny has handled the purse before, dispatched by his mother to retrieve it on more than a few occasions, but he has never laid hands on it without authorization. He has certainly never opened it. He drags it by the strap from beneath the bed. He doesn't remember it ever being so heavy. He heaves the purse onto the mattress and sits down next to it. The burgundy vinyl is smooth. A long flap like a flat, wide tongue covers nearly the entirety of one side. He unsnaps the flap with a yank and flips it over, revealing an interior zipper. He tugs it open.

The purse interior fans open into three compartments. Each section is topped with what looks like at least half a box's worth of loose tissue. Danny removes them in three bunches and, with both hands, places them gently on the bed, careful to keep the stacks intact.

His attention is drawn first to the purse's middle compartment. Inside lies a bounty of individually-wrapped restaurant breadbasket fare: saltine crackers, Melba Toasts, breadsticks, plus a slew of little butter containers. Danny glances toward the closed bathroom door. He rips open a package of Melba Toast, bites and stuffs until it's all in his mouth. He slips the wrapper into the back pocket of his jeans.

Chewing, Danny checks the compartment to the left of the middle breadbasket section. There he finds his mother's wallet, the lining ripped slightly on one side, some important-looking, folded papers, five little motel soaps, a tube of lip balm and a vial of tiny, orange pills. A few coins, some sugar packets and loose linty sesame seeds line the bottom.

The third compartment is far more interesting. Danny fishes out a package of chocolate chips, nearly half-full. He unfolds the opened end and shakes out a handful of chocolate, pops them all in his mouth at once. The remnants of Melba Toast stuck in his teeth add a surprisingly pleasing crunch. He returns his attention to the purse, examines the rest of the last compartment. "The dessert section," Danny thinks. A package of sweetened coconut, three Halloween-size Kit-Kats, Baker's semi-sweet chocolate and something wrapped in a white, grease-stained paper napkin. Danny grabs the curious napkin, unwraps it, and finds, stacked upon each other, two almond cookies from the Chinese buffet the family ate at a week ago. Danny remembers eating eight such cookies himself that night. He sniffs them and salivates. He knows detection is almost certain if he removes one of the cookies to eat it. Still, he reasons, his mother might blame his father — she blames a lot of things on him. But that would mean a big fight, and a big fight is almost worse than no cookie. Danny has an epiphany. He decides to take both cookies, gambling that the absence of both will simply allow them to be forgotten.

The water stops running in the bathroom. Danny hears the dull rattle of the shower curtain, then his mother's voice, bellowing. "Turn that TV down! We're going to get thrown out of here, it's so loud!" Danny quickly wraps the two cookies in their napkin and tucks the bundle beneath his shirt, wedges it in his left armpit, upper arm held tight against his flank. The television is blasting an outlandishly upbeat, strangely beguiling jingle about cheese. *Cheese, glorious cheese, so sumptuous and luscious.* There is pounding on the bathroom wall. "Turn that down now!" *Cheese, marvellous cheese, makes everything scrumptious.* Danny replaces the tissues in the purse, hastily distributing them among the three sections. "Don't make me come out there! I'm soaking wet and you'll be sorry!" *What else is so versatile? Real cheese, it's always a hit!* Danny's breathing accelerates. He works the purse zipper and starts on the flap. "That's it! You're in for it!" *It's cheese! Marvellous cheese!* The button on the flap is not as easy to fasten as it was to open. Danny's fingers feel pudgy and clumsy as he attempts to guide the little knob protruding from one of the discs into the seemingly smaller hole on the other. He catches the tip of his thumb and winces. Footsteps boom on the bathroom floor. *Versatile cheese! Glorious cheese!* Danny's next attempt produces a satisfying snap and the purse is closed. He drops to the floor and shoves it beneath the bed, then climbs back up onto the bed, lies on his back and closes his eyes. The bathroom door bursts open as the cheese commercial arrives at its big finish, topped off by an enthusiastic announcer's voiceover. *Make your meals sing with real cheese.*

Danny listens to his mother march into the room. The television is shut off just as the Spider-Man reintroduction music starts up. His mother is livid. "Give me a break! I can tell by your breathing you're not sleeping." She chases him from the bed with a shake of the mattress. "What the hell were you doing?" She has a white motel towel wrapped tightly around her torso and another around the top of her head like a turban.

Danny slinks to the other end of the room, the lump of cookies under his arm. He is convinced he'll be caught.

"Just get out of here for a while. Go play outside. Get some fresh air." His mother sits down on the edge of the bed, her back to Danny. "Come back in half in hour. Let me do my hair in peace and quiet."

Relieved, Danny snatches his toy gun from the floor. By the time he passes his mother on his way to the door, she has her purse up on the bed, leaning against her hip. She is digging through it. The fear is hot in Danny's chest.

"Here. Take this." Leandra waves a package of two breadsticks at him. He reaches to accept it with his gun-toting hand. "Don't point that thing at me!"

"Mom, it's just a toy."

"It looks so real. It creeps me out."

Danny transfers the gun to his other hand, stiffly, careful of the cookies in his armpit. He takes the snack with his newly-freed hand.

"What's wrong with your arm?"

"Nothing!" Danny scurries to the door and slips out. His mother calls him back but he ignores her and runs down the hall, knowing she won't follow dressed in towels. Outside, he removes the plunder from under his arm. Crumbs roll down his trunk. The cookies are a little broken but quite edible. And delicious. Danny wolfs them down where he stands.

THE TALE OF DONKEY KONG JUNIOR

Bob did try, once, to tell Danny. Only a few weeks back. They were across the table from each other in a plastic McDonald's booth. Between them their lunch. One and a half regular hamburgers each, a shared small fry, and two glasses of water. Danny's extracted pickles lay glutinous and ostracized on one of the flattened wrinkled paper wrappers.

"Want to hear a story?"

"What's it about?"

"This is the story of Donkey Kong. And his son, Donkey Kong Junior."

"They're donkeys?"

"No, actually. Gorillas."

"Gorillas?"

"Like King Kong. Only, Donkey."

"Is this a movie?"

Bob was unsure how to answer. He gnawed on a French fry. "It could be a movie."

"It's going to be a movie?"

"It could be one." He tried to be vague. "Some day."

"So, what about it?"

"In the beginning is a kidnapping. Donkey Kong kidnaps a beautiful blonde woman and carries her away."

"Sounds like King Kong."

"But it's different. This is just the beginning part. The good part comes after." Bob sipped at his water. "So, the gorilla takes the beautiful blonde. And her boyfriend, Mario, sets off to rescue her. The gorilla holes up with the lady in an abandoned barrel factory and when Mario finds them there, he throws the barrels at Mario."

"He throws…barrels?"

"Some of the barrels are on fire."

"Okay."

"Anyway, eventually, Mario gets his girlfriend back, and then he captures Donkey Kong. Sticks him in a cage."

"A cage? How big?"

"I don't know, a gorilla-sized cage."

"But isn't he big like King Kong?"

"No, he's big like a regular gorilla. Just the name is like King Kong." Bob paused for a bite of hamburger. "Anyway, listen. This is where it gets interesting. After he's captured, Donkey Kong's son, Donkey Kong Junior, goes into action to save his dad from Mario."

"Does Donkey Kong Junior throw barrels, too?"

"No!" Bob voice boomed, much louder than he intended. Danny stared back at him with eyes a little wider. "Sorry about that. But, no. Junior doesn't throw barrels. He knocks fruit off of vines."

"What?"

"He knocks fruit off of vines so that it falls on the creatures that Mario sends out after him. When the creatures get hit by a fruit, they disappear. And Junior has to get keys. To get his dad out of the cage."

"Dad?"

"Yes Danny?"

"Are you making this up?"

"Making it up? No."

"So, when is this movie coming out anyway?"

"It's not a movie!"

"A book?"

Bob sighed. He flopped his hamburger upside down onto its paper wrapper. A crinkling sound on the table. The uniformity of the bun's underside was marred by a small, shallow crater of flour. The tip of Bob's pinkie finger fit inside it. He dug out some of the clumpy flour with the edge of his nail. Bit at it. He reached into his pocket and pulled out his change. Seventeen cents. "Do you have any money on you?"

"Me?"

"A dime? Anything?"

"I don't have any money, Dad."

That makes two of us, Bob thought.

A BOY AND HIS GUN

Danny crouches inside a cedar hedge that runs the length of the path that connects the main building of the motel and the swimming pool. He is draped by the thin, bare branches in the centre of the hedge. Beneath his feet the ground is soft. A cushioning layer of dead and browned strands of cedar leaves lies atop the dry earth. His view of the path is partially obstructed, but then so is the view of him from the path. All the easier to pick off unsuspecting passersby with his gun.

When they put all of their stuff into storage before moving into the motel, Danny was allowed to keep one of his things. To occupy himself with. He wanted to bring a lot more, but his mother said no way to the box he filled with toys and comics from his room. He begged and pleaded. "But it *is* one thing. One box." His mother was impatient, got irritated fast. One thing or nothing, she threatened. Danny chose his toy revolver.

"Please, not that. Can't you bring something nice?"

Danny protested.

"Why don't you bring one of your comics?"

"I'll get bored!"

"We're not going to be there that long. Don't bring that gun. I hate that thing."

"But *I* like it. Please, Mom! I won't be loud."

"Why don't you just let him bring it?" Bob entered the room. He started dragging Danny's mattress toward the door. "He likes the gun."

Leandra glowered at Bob. "Why don't you stay out of it? I'm the one that's going to have to stay with him, listening to that *bang-bang-bang*, and the *pow-pow-pow*, while you're gallivanting around town."

"Looking for work."

"Well, you should have already had work, and you should have paid the fucking rent, so we wouldn't be off to live in a fleabag motel."

Bob hauled the mattress through the door. Leandra followed behind, not quite finished. "To a fleabag motel with our *son!*"

Danny cringed. He didn't like being used as leverage one way or the other in his parents' fights. It made him feel guilty somehow. But, he realized, the gun issue appeared to be resolved. And, sure enough, it wasn't mentioned again. His mother either forgot or gave up trying to keep him from bringing it along.

The best thing about the gun is that the cylinder actually pops out and, with a flick of the finger, can be spun. Danny does this each time he picks off an unsuspecting innocent on the path beside the cedar hedge, pretending to reload his gun. The barrel is metallic black, the handle brown. Danny is silent in the hedge. Nobody sees him. Nobody has any idea they are being riddled with sniper's bullets.

He hears footsteps coming up the path. A new victim. It's an older man in a big straw sun hat, beige shirt and beige shorts. He is fishing in his pocket as he passes Danny. "Bang," Danny whispers. The man pulls a room key from his shorts pocket. There's a little ping on the pavement of the path. The man keeps walking. Danny spies a coin. He waits for the man to be clear of the path. He parts firm cedar leaves and crawls a little bit from the hedge, his legs still inside of it. It's a quarter. Danny reaches for it and claims it.

"Hey! What are you doing there?"

Danny hears the voice, a man's, gruff and angry, but can't see the person producing it.

"You're not supposed to be in there! Get out of those hedges!"

Danny obeys. The hedge snaps a little as he exits. He spins around twice but still cannot see who is yelling at him.

"You're in big trouble, young man! You wait there and we're going to go talk to your parents."

A chill nestles coldly along the edges of Danny's collarbone and shoulders. Still unaware of where the voice is coming from, he begins to run toward the main building.

"Stop right there!" The voice seems to be coming, strangely, from above. Danny looks up. Peering over the edge of the main building's roof, the motel janitor is shaking a fist at him from two storeys up. Danny has seen him around before, lugging garbage bags to the container in the parking lot. Sweeping up empty potato chip bags and cigarette butts off the motel grounds. "Wait there, I'm coming down. Don't try and run off." Danny doesn't even think, he just aims. Pulls the trigger. Feigns recoil. The janitor's eyes are daggers, even angrier than before. He scurries from sight, and Danny sprints up the path, toward the main building, the rooms. His heart beats in his throat.

UNDULATING NECK FAT

Bob is fifteen, twenty years older than almost everyone else in the arcade. The lights are dim; seedy and comfortable at the same time. There is a clamour of conversation, bleeps and blasts. A young couple engages in a passionate session of dry humping between the Galaga and Frogger machines. Bob is comfortable in the arcade. There are lots of people, and almost all of them are focused on their own thing, their own games.

He makes his way to the change machine. Inserts a twenty. The machine pulls his bill in with a whir. Rejects it with the same sound. The twenty dangles like a worn-out tongue. Bob tries again. Same result.

There is a small counter in the middle of the arcade. A handwritten cardboard sign hangs in front of it from two pieces of masking tape. ABSOLUTELY NO REFUNDS. Behind the counter, on a backless stool, sits a fat man in a maroon turtleneck. His arms are crossed, hugging his breasts. He has a few wisps of white hair left on his shiny head. A toothpick wedged in the corner of his mouth, only the point exposed. His flabby chin and undulating neck fat are one, hanging from his face like a short bib.

"I couldn't get change for this from the machine."

"Doesn't take twenties." The arcade owner straightens slightly and reaches into his left pants pocket. He pulls out a wad of bills, unfolds two tens. He flattens them with the palm of his large hand on top of the counter. "These'll work."

"Thanks."

Bob injects the first ten into the change machine and listens to the quarters plink down into the dispenser. His fingers twitch and his heart beats a little faster. He feels a few eyes on him. His large load of change has attracted some attention. He inserts the second ten dollar bill. The rain of coins sounds duller this time, falling on top of his first set of quarters. Bob reaches for the dispenser and pushes gently on the metal flap. It won't budge. He tries again. It's stuck. Up against a wall of quarters inside. He tries to pull the flap out, but his fingers are either too large or too clumsy, his nails too stumpy.

"I can't get to my change."

The arcade owner extracts himself from his stool and waddles over to the change machine. He jabs the immovable dispenser flap with his forefinger.

"Did you put both tens in?"

"Yes."

"Did you take the quarters out before you put the second one in?"

"No."

"The machine doesn't take twenties. So there's no room for twenty dollars worth of quarters."

"My money—"

"I'll get it. Hang on. Just hang on."

The owner pulls a penknife out of his pocket. With great concentration, he unfolds a blade with the edge of a fingernail. He stabs the change machine right between the bottom edge of the flap and the base of the dispenser. Roots around. He jerks his hand to the left, to the right. And again. The blade forces a few quarters free. One spins as it hits the hard floor. The owner switches tactics and thrusts the blade in and out until the quarters start dropping from the dispenser at, to Bob, an alarming rate.

"I think I'm okay now." Bob goes down on one knee and pinches a quarter between his thumb and forefinger. He grabs another. He looks around, protective of his hoard. The quarters are still dropping. "Okay, I'm good."

"Yeah." The owner shuffles away. Over his shoulder, irritated, "Don't do that again."

Bob fumes. He feels he's been spoken to as if he is one of the kids in denim jackets with Deep Purple written on the back in marker and jeans so tight the separation of their testicles shows. He erases that thought from his mind. He picks up the remaining quarters from the floor and rises, empties the dispenser. Weighs his pockets down with the coins.

Bob mopes away from the change machine. Though he's sure he's being watched, he resists looking in the direction of the owner's counter. His mood lightens the closer he gets to the Donkey Kong Junior machine. He pats the outsides of his front pockets with the palms of his hands, jangling the mounds of change inside each one. Soft quills of anticipation tickle his shoulders.

He steps before the Donkey Kong Junior machine. The demonstration mode is running. Bob watches the phantom play transpire on the screen – Junior climbing vines – and fishes out a quarter from his pocket. He taps the coin against the control panel. The pretend player loses Junior to a red Snapjaw and the title screen pops up. The colours and font are stirring. Finally, the high score screen appears. Panic shortens Bob's breath. Two spots of perspiration chill his underarms. Somebody named ABE has bested his high score.

CONFISCATION

Danny raps frantically at the room door. Glances down the hall. No sign of the janitor. His mother opens the door halfway. "What are you doing back already? Come back later."

Danny squeezes past her. "Close the door!"

"What?"

"Close the door!"

She complies. Takes a step toward Danny but stops up. There is thunderous knocking at their door.

"Don't open it! Please!"

"Danny, really." Leandra opens the door. The janitor pops his head in, looks around, points in at Danny. "Hah! You thought I didn't know your room number? I know where everybody's staying!"

"Excuse me," Leandra grumbles. She looks back at Danny, eyes cold. "What is going on here?"

"That kid of yours pointed his gun at me. Going to get himself into trouble with that thing."

Leandra looks appalled. She stretches out her hand, palm up. "Hand it over."

"But, Mom! It's just a toy!"

"I don't care. I told you that thing gives me the creeps, now hand it over before you go and get yourself shot for real."

"I'd of shot him," the janitor offers.

Leandra begins shutting the door, not waiting for the janitor to clear the entranceway. He totters backwards. "Thank you," Leandra says into the crack of remaining open doorway. "I'll take care of this. He won't bother you anymore. Sorry for your trouble, have a good day." She closes the door completely. Turns. Puts out her hand again. "Give."

"Aw, Mom. "

"Hand it over. Now."

"Please? One more chance?"

"No way. Give it to me. I should have never let you bring that thing along in the first place."

Danny surrenders his gun to Leandra. She finds a spot for it in her purse.

"Now I've *really* got nothing to do."

"Here. Have a Melba Toast."

HONEST ABE

Sick to his stomach, Bob staggers from the arcade. He squints in the bright light of the mall. He can't believe his score has been beaten. And done so soon. He makes his way past a magazine and newspaper kiosk, a shoe store, a plus-size clothing store. A few steps from the food court he finds the pharmacy connected to the walk-in clinic.

Inside, he purchases a bottle of Pepto Bismol. The cashier bags it in a brown paper bag that isn't much larger than the medicine. Bob shuffles out of the pharmacy, to the centre of the mall corridor, and leans his back against a fake tree. He reaches into the bag and unscrews the cap on the Pepto Bismal bottle. He crumples the top of the bag a bit, to expose the spout of the bottle, and raises the whole thing to his lips. He takes a swig. The sickly sweet, thick liquid seeps down the inside of his throat, down to his stomach, luxuriously coating everything in its path. Bob sighs audibly. A pair of ladies passing by point and shake their heads.

Bob returns to the arcade, his stomach somewhat settled, intent on regaining the Donkey Kong Junior high score. The owner spots him from his perch behind the Absolutely No Refunds desk.

"Hey! You can't bring that stuff in here!"

Bob reaches into the brown paper bag and pulls out the bottle of Pepto Bismol. He holds it by the cap with two fingers and a thumb. Dangles it.

The arcade owner gives him a dismissive wave of the hand, shakes his head. "Just keep it out of sight. Look like a damned dirty drunk. Carousing in my place."

Bob stuffs the medicine, paper bag and all, into the back pocket of his jeans. He feels the outsides of his front pockets, loaded with quarters. The Donkey Kong Junior machine stands unoccupied at the back of the room. Waiting for him.

He stares again at the high score screen. BOB has been relegated to the fifth best high score. ABE occupies the first, second, third, and fourth spots.

Bob can't help but imagine ABE as Abraham Lincoln himself, stovepipe hat and all, stoically guiding Junior past Snapjaws, dropping fruit on Nitpicker birds, negotiating moving platforms, jumping fiery Sparks. He pictures a crowd gathered around the Donkey Kong Junior machine, fan-waving ladies in petticoats and boys in Union frocks and caps, politely applauding President Lincoln's every triumph, every completed screen. His experience and leadership, his masterful debating skills, his war-steeled nerves, his courage displayed in the face of pro-slavery elements; all unfair advantages against Bob. Abe Lincoln can probably rescue Donkey Kong from the clutches of Mario with one hand while penning with the other a stirring oration for rousing delivery at Jonesborough or some other battlefield. And nearby a stack of raw onion sandwiches on a round, dark brown Biedermeier pedestal table, brought in special at the President's request.

Bob feels toyed with. This ABE person beat his high score four times. Surely had ABE wished, he could have easily eclipsed Bob's score one more time. ABE could have had all five slots to himself, a clean sweep of the high score screen. But ABE has left one BOB score intact, and in the fifth position at that. Bob is convinced ABE is mocking him. Goading him. With onion breath.

Assassination in his heart, Bob inserts his first quarter of the day.

LEDGE

"Yes you *could* swim in your underwear. Nobody's going to notice. Nobody's going to care."

"I won't!"

"Fine, then we're staying right here in the room."

"But, Mom, you should have brought my bathing suit."

"I didn't know this place was going to have a pool, and I didn't know we were going to be here this long. Why don't we just go down to the pool? Look: if there are people, you don't have to swim. But if we're the only ones there, you could swim in your underwear. And nobody will see you."

"You could have at least packed me some shorts."

"I wasn't thinking straight. I'm sorry. Now quiet for a minute, I want to hear this." Leandra motions at the television, *The Guiding Light*. Some old man lying in a hospital bed, a few concerned-looking people gathered around him.

"Could I *please* have my gun back? I won't point it at anybody, I promise!"

"Shhh."

Danny mopes to the bathroom, closes the door. He pulls open the shower curtain and sits on the edge of the bathtub, buries his face in his hands. He has never felt so bored. Stands again and, one hand leaning on the tiled wall, he steps up onto the bathtub ledge. He stretches his arms out straight on either side of himself, walks the imaginary tightrope. Four steps and he's all the way across. He pivots to repeat the feat in the other direction but teeters slightly, off balance. Instinctively, he reaches up with one hand, grasps the shower curtain rod, which snaps in two with a crack. Danny falls. His forehead thumps against the bathtub ledge and he winds up in a sitting position on the floor. His head tingles. He feels a drip on the bridge of his nose. Another, and rather wet.

Leandra bursts into the bathroom. Danny's face is a red mess of blood. More pools on the floor before him. A tremor like electricity courses through her from her head to the pit of her stomach. "My baby!"

WASTING QUARTERS

Bob isn't sharp. His mind is ahead of his fingers, on the high score list instead of on the vines, platforms and chains. He isn't paying attention to the work it takes to achieve a high score and he's wasting quarters.

Donkey Kong Junior consists of four different screens. Once Bob completes all four, culminating in Donkey Kong's rescue by Junior, the cycle starts over, repeating itself with ever-increasing difficulty. The first two times through the screens are little more than a pattern to Bob. Moves and jumps memorized, perfected through repetition. It's after the second liberation of Donkey Kong that the game becomes interesting. It's back to the vines and Snapjaws are everywhere. But a mental picture of the high score screen, the name ABE in the top four slots, clouds Bob's vision. He stupidly allows Junior to walk off a ledge and fall into the water. A mistake even a beginner wouldn't make. GAME OVER. Furious, Bob bites his lip and punches the screen, fist turned sideways.

"Hey! I saw that!" The arcade owner hobbles over. His great girth swings side to side. "You want to get yourself thrown out?"

"Okay. Yeah. Sorry."

"Christ, you're worse than the kids, you take this so seriously."

"Okay." Bob slides another quarter into the coin slot. The start-up sequence begins. Donkey Kong is encaged. Mario and somebody that looks exactly like Mario hoist the great ape to the top of the screen with ropes and pulleys. GET KEY FROM MARIO. SAVE YOUR PAPA!

"No wonder you drink that pink shit like it's water. Going to put yourself in the hospital, you are."

Bob isn't listening. The game has started again. This time he'll be vigilant. He won't let himself die foolishly. He'll erase all traces of ABE.

AN ABUNDANCE OF BLOOD

Using every clean towel in the bathroom, Leandra manages to clean enough blood off of Danny's face to find the source of the seepage on his forehead, an inch-long gash. She wets a facecloth and holds it to it, applies pressure. The blood is everywhere. On her hands, up her arms, on Danny's hands and arms, his shirt and pants. A small pool on the floor. Hundreds of tiny red spots dot the exterior of the bathtub in a dense pattern.

"Looks like somebody got murdered in here," Danny says.

"Don't joke!"

Danny laughs and cries at the same time. For a few seconds his teeth chatter.

"You're going to be okay, Danny. We have to go to the clinic, you're going to need stitches. Let's try and get up."

"Stitches? I don't want stitches!" Danny has never had stitches.

"We'll see what they say. Now you hold the towel." She directs his hand to the facecloth, presses his hand against it flat. She stands, offers her hand, helps Danny up. "Can you walk?"

He feels quite good, though his forehead stings beneath the facecloth. "I'm okay." He catches a glimpse of himself in the mirror. He cannot believe he is the boy covered in blood. He follows his mother out of the bathroom and waits for her by the motel room door. She retrieves her purse from beneath her bed and they are off.

Leandra props her left arm against Danny's back, her hand on his hip. She reaches across herself with her other hand and clutches Danny's right hand. "Keep that towel on your forehead. Press on it." She escorts him this way from the main motel building and down the cedar hedge path. In the sunlight, Danny's appearance is grislier, somehow bloodier. Leandra is thankful his spirits are good. She tells herself it's going to be okay. That cuts to the head just bleed more, it's natural. It just doesn't look natural, doesn't feel natural to see her son in a bloodied state.

Near the pool gate they encounter the janitor, an empty Pepsi bottle with a pale, sun-bleached label in his hand. He watches them pass, mouth agape, his eyes wide, perplexed. The spite is acrid in Leandra's throat. The smallest hint of a smile, however, crawls to life in one corner of her mouth.

"He got shot. Are you happy now?"

NO REFUNDS

After his tenth game, Bob finds his groove and goes on a roll. The games before were throwaways, warm-ups. To get the kinks out. It is a long grind to get past the 30,000-point mark, but he is enjoying the journey. There is a knife of pain stabbing at the left side of his neck and shoulders. He can't turn his head in that direction. The loose web of skin between his left forefinger and thumb is raw. His right index finger – his jump finger – is sore. He ignores the discomfort; by game 15 he has managed to surpass his personal best score and make a dent in ABE's dominance of the high score screen.

INSERT COIN

PLAYER	COIN
1	1
2	2

RANK	SCORE	NAME
1ST	043500	ABE
2ND	040200	BOB
3RD	038950	BOB
4TH	038100	BOB
5TH	036850	ABE

Bob backs away from the control panel before commencing his next game. Cracks his knuckles. Stretches out his arms. Shakes his fingers. He's got hunger pangs like his stomach is being eaten from the inside. He steps forward. Removes a quarter from his pocket. Slips it into the coin slot. Instead of the melodic game startup he expects, however, he hears a hallow ping. His quarter didn't work.

He digs it from the coin return and tries again. This time nothing at all; no startup, no ping. Bob depresses the square plastic casing surrounding the coin slot and his quarter is released to the coin return. Bob pockets it and tries a different quarter. Again, it's caught. His frustration grows. He presses the coin slot to no result. He pushes and releases it, over and over in quick succession. The machine won't give back his quarter. With both hands, simultaneously, he slaps the sides of the machine down low, abreast of the coin slot area.

"Hey! You trying to break my machine?"

Bob ignores the owner and tries out a series of random slaps, punches and crude karate chops on various parts of the video game machine.

"I said hey!" The owner pulls him by the shoulder, turns him around.

"It ate my quarter."

"That's what they all say." The toothpick bobs between his pudgy lips.

"No, it really did eat my quarter."

"So put in another one. You've got plenty."

"I want my quarter back."

"You've seen the sign. Everybody sees the sign. No refunds. Never."

"I want my quarter back and I want it back now." Bob edges closer to the owner.

"You're going to get yourself thrown out of here, mister."

"I want my quarter back and I want it back now." Bob plants his face an inch from the owner's. The toothpick almost grazes his chin. "I didn't get my game. Give me my quarter back."

"Get out of my shop. Get out or I'll call the cops."

Bob's heart is racing, the skin on his face prickling. "Give me my quarter back."

The owner spins in his tracks. "All right! That's it! I am calling the cops."

"Excellent," Bob sings, mockingly. He folds his arms, leans back on the Donkey Kong Junior machine, and waits.

IMPORTANT

Leandra focuses on the sidewalk beneath her feet, silently counting each rectangular slab of cement. The four lanes of rumbling cars and trucks beside her are merely noise. As they make their way to the clinic, she has decided to only allow herself to look at Danny once every twenty sidewalk sections. A small part of her fantasizes his in-jury and the blood will vanish while she isn't looking. She'll count up to twenty and look up to find her son healed by some unseen hand. She permits the fantasy to expand. The unseen hand will not only mend Danny's wound, but will also deliver them from turmoil and bring a measure of order to their lives. In her mind, the unseen hand begins to grow. Then, in slow stages, turn light green. The hand be-comes more than just an appendage: it gains an arm, a torso, a body. A face. It is Lou Ferrigno as The Incredible Hulk. He looks from side to side, bares his teeth and growls. Leandra marvels at his massive green arms. A kernel of hope stirs within her. It feels like surprise. Like Christmas in July. But instead of rescuing Leandra, The Hulk only turns and runs away in slow motion, the remaining shreds of a torn white shirt flapping lightly against his chiselled deltoids and triceps.

Danny feels oddly happy. He certainly isn't bored anymore. His forehead still stings, but along with the pain comes a certain pride of ownership. The thought occurs to him for the first time since the fall that he hasn't cried yet. And he doesn't particularly feel like it. The prospect of stitches in his forehead is suddenly extremely appealing. Battle scars to signify survival. Infallible proof of it etched into his skin. The sun is bright and there's a breeze. He holds his shoulders a little straighter.

Danny spies a woman pushing a baby carriage ahead, coming along the sidewalk toward him and his mother. He adjusts his trajectory by stepping slightly to the left. His mother tugs him back to her side. He glances at her. She is looking down at the sidewalk. The lady with the baby carriage is getting closer. Danny pulls to the left again, but again his move is resisted. "Mom!"

"Just a minute." His mother won't look up. She keeps walking.

The baby carriage is before them and Danny stops in his tracks. His mother, a step ahead of him now, eyes still on the ground, tries to drag him alongside her. He wrests his arm from Leandra's grip, stands his ground. She finally looks up.

The young lady with the baby carriage is wearing a red track suit. Blond hair pulled back on her head in a long ponytail. She has one hand over her mouth. She stares at Danny with eyes wide.

Leandra glances back at her son. The blood stains on his face, arms and clothes are drying, darkening. His appearance makes her think of child soldiers from another era who faked their age to get into combat. It makes her nauseous.

"Do you need help?" the young mother asks from behind her carriage.

Leandra only stares at her. Her stomach on the edge of revolt.

Danny steps forward. "It looks worse than it really is." He gently grips his mother's arm at the elbow and nudges her ahead. With a bob of his chin he indicates the shopping mall across the street. "We're just going to the clinic."

Danny leads his mother around the baby carriage and to the end of the block. When the Walk signal appears he escorts her across the street. They enter the parking lot of the mall and for the first time in a very long time Danny feels important.

ALTERCATION

The arcade owner is seething. Ice in his eyes as he stares Bob down from behind his desk. His Absolutely No Refunds desk. His toothpick is ground and frayed. "Ten minutes, mister," he shouts. "The police will be here in ten minutes."

Bob stares right back, still leaning back against the Donkey Kong Junior machine. The urge to play a game while he waits for the police to arrive is nearly too powerful to resist. But he wants to be ready when the police arrive. To present his side of the story and get his quarter back.

A teenager with a dark brown mullet, jeans ripped in the knees and a Judas Priest T-shirt approaches Bob, stares right at him. He's got a cigarette tucked behind one ear. Bob looks to one side, the other. There is nobody else for the kid to be looking at. "Can I get on that game, mister?"

Bob doesn't react. The kid slips a hand into his jeans pocket and withdraws a quarter. Motions at the machine with it. Bob stands up straight, puts both hands up in front of his chest. "I'm on this machine. It ate my quarter and I'm waiting to get it back."

"Now what's going on?" the arcade owner growls. He shuffles over, eyes the quarter in the kid's hand. "You want to play this game?"

"Yeah, but it's no big deal, man."

"Move over you bastard," the owner barks at Bob. "There's a customer wants to play."

"Give me back my quarter. I will not talk to you until you give me my refund. I paid my money and I did not get my game. Give me back—"

The owner lunges at Bob, faster than seemingly possible for a man of his size. His hands are on Bob's collarbone, fingers pressing. Bob turns his body sideways, into the Donkey Kong Junior machine, to escape his grasp, but the owner grabs him by the waist and pulls. Bob grasps the joystick with his left hand, then clasps his left hand with his right, forming something of a clamp. He puts his head down, digs his chin into his chest and braces himself. The owner prods with his fingers into the waistline of the back of Bob's pants and tugs. There is ripping and the tugging ceases for a moment. Bob turns his head for a quick look. The owner is charging again, coming at him with arms extended, fingers bent like claws. Bob removes his hands from the joystick and hugs the Donkey Kong Junior machine, squeezing tight with his arms. He feels the owner's hands squeeze under his own armpits and he is yanked, hands flat against his chest. Bob's fingers ache, pressing hard against the back paneling. His palms sting where they push into the straight edge of the cabinet's corners. He feels the machine give. The back end leaves the floor for an instant and drops back down. He won't let go. The arcade owner pulls and pulls at him. The machine lifts up again in the back and settles back down hard with a thump and a jangle of coins. Bob's nose painfully grinds into the screen. The owner is on him again quickly, pulling harder than before. Bob feels the machine's back end rise, followed by an eerie, momentary sensation of weightlessness when it reaches its tipping point. Donkey Kong Junior is coming down hard and fast on top of him. He lets go of the machine and throws himself to the side, hits the ground painfully shoulder-first. The arcade owner falls next to him. With a great thwack, the Donkey Kong Junior machine crashes to the ground inches from their bodies.

"Holy shit," the teenager utters. "That is fucked up."

FAMILY REUNION

Her stomach settled somewhat, Leandra holds one of the glass doors outside the mall open for Danny and they go inside. Without stopping, she unsnaps the flap on her purse and gazes down to unzip it. She wants to have Danny's Medicare card ready the instant they walk into the clinic. She finds Danny's toy gun wedged up tight against her wallet. She removes the gun with her right hand and reaches for the wallet with her left. Suddenly she is walking into Danny, who has stopped right in the middle of the mall corridor.

He is staring at something off to their right. With nervous wonder in his voice, he says, "It's Dad."

It's a scene Leandra cannot comprehend. A fat middle-aged man is pulling her husband, who is lying face down on the ground, by the ankles, out of a video arcade. A throng of teenagers crowds the arcade entrance, laughing, hooting. Bob has only one shoe on. He is swimming a bastardized version of the front crawl on the ground, digging his fingers into the floor, trying, in vain, to get back into the arcade. The fat man's pants stretch to their tightest limit in the ass area as he squats for extra leverage. Bob kicks free and scrambles to his feet. The man tackles Bob to the floor again. The teenagers cheer.

"Mom?"

Leandra feels outside of herself. It can't be Bob, she tells herself. He's delivering phone books. It can't be Bob, she tells herself. This person who resembles her husband has one shoe on and is desperate to get inside a video arcade.

"Mom? What's happening to Dad?"

Bob and the arcade owner grapple with each other on the floor. The owner scrambles on top and places his hand over Bob's face. He begins to squeeze. Bob squeals, feet thrashing air. The back of his head is shoved hard against the floor. Bob shakes and spins, breaks free, and crawls a few paces toward the arcade before being jumped on again.

Leandra's head is hot now. She is furious. At the man attacking her husband. At Bob. At the ridiculous, frightening situation. She marches swiftly to the skirmish, her arms swinging with anger. Two teenage boys near the front of the crowd point at her. They turn into the mass behind them and push their way inside the arcade. Then the whole pack falls back, screaming. Some crouch to the ground, arms covering their heads.

Danny, one hand still holding the bloody facecloth to his forehead, watches his mother enter the fray. He sees the toy revolver in her hand, makes the connection between it and the panicking kids in the arcade. He's scared for her and follows her path, running.

"Get off of him!" Leandra screams. The arcade owner turns, looks directly at her right hand. Fear crawls across his face. He rolls off of Bob, crawls backwards like an elephantine crab. His eyes constantly on Leandra's hand.

Leandra looks to where the man is staring. She sees the gun. She smiles, wide. Begins to snicker. A wild cackle escapes her lips. She has a quick look at Bob. He's on his hands and knees, gazing up at her, baffled. Leandra raises the gun, clasps it between both of her hands and points it straight-armed at the fat man's head. "No!" he screams, arms crossed in front of his face. The crowd of teenagers shrieks. Leandra giggles.

"Leandra?" She revolves one half turn in Bob's direction, her feet sliding neatly on the floor, her arms still stiff. The toy gun is pointed at her husband. "Leandra? What are you doing?"

"Shut up! Everybody shut up! What the fuck is going on? What the fuck?"

Danny sidles up beside his mother. The few remaining teenagers, the diehards, cowering at the edges of the arcade entrance, gasp collectively at the sight of him. He puts a hand on his mother's shoulder. She twists her head to look at him, gun still aimed at Bob. Her face softens. She smiles at her son. "Just a minute, honey," she coos. "I'm doing something."

Beyond his mother, down the corridor, Danny spots two blue-uniformed policemen as they round the corner. One of them points at the scene, alarm registered on his face. He bursts into a sprint, hand on his holster. The second cop jogs behind his partner, a walkie-talkie to his mouth. Danny takes a step back, staggered. "Mom, really."

Leandra's expression changes to curiosity. She studies Danny's face momentarily, then turns away, to look where he's looking. She's bowled over violently by the lead cop. The revolver flies from her hand, hits the ground and slides along the floor. It comes to rest before the arcade entrance. The teenagers materialize from their hiding places and timidly encircle the toy.

"Don't anybody touch that!" the second police officer barks. The crowd recoils as one.

Danny's mother is lying face down on the floor, the first cop sitting on her backside. He cuffs her hands behind her back. Leandra is screaming. Danny looks to his father. He is crying. The fat man on the floor spits at him and scrambles to his feet. With both arms raised in the air, he renews his attack. The second police officer intervenes quickly, stepping between the two men. He and the fat man struggle.

Danny feels an onslaught of tears surfacing. His teeth chatter again, like in the bathroom at the motel. He inhales a big breath. Sniffs it all back. Walks between his parents, toward the arcade entrance. The teenagers retreat further into the arcade. Danny bends down and picks up the gun.

"Drop that!" shouts the second policeman. Danny turns, the toy gun dangling on one finger by the trigger casing. The policeman steps in front of the fat man, who is now cuffed. "Drop that, son. Drop it and back away."

"It's not real," Danny says. "It's a toy."

The police officer draws his own gun. Points it at Danny. "Just do what I say, son. Drop that weapon."

They aren't listening to him. "No, really," Danny pleads. "You don't understand. This is all a mistake. This is a toy gun. This is my toy gun."

The first cop has his firearm aimed at Danny now, as well. "Drop it!" he barks. "Drop it and it'll be okay."

Danny surveys the unimaginable scene. Two policemen aiming guns at him. His mother handcuffed and prostrate on the ground. His father also on the floor, sobbing, one shoe missing. In one of his own hands a blood-soaked motel room facecloth, in the other his toy revolver. He raises the gun, presses the business end to his temple. He pulls the trigger and listens to the quiet click. "Bang," he whispers.

Danny chucks the gun, underhand, to the floor in front of him. It lands between his parents.

"It's not real," he wails. "It's just not real."

THE KETCHUP
WE WERE BORN WITH

Parker was born eleven years after the fourth epidemic of Mad Cow Disease, so he wasn't subject to the decade-long interim of confusion and recovery. He didn't take part in the endless Land and Casualty Surveys, argue in any Estates-General debates, nor was he a signatory to The Charter of Rations. Everything was already set up by the time Parker was born. He didn't have to worry. Stored in a warehouse near his home were his 100 litres of ketchup; his allocation for life.

Two weeks before his eighth birthday, Parker was up in a tree playing Robins and Orioles with friends. Just when it became his turn to be the momma bird, Parker fell out of the tree and died. He hadn't even touched his ketchup.

Forty-seven people perished in the ensuing mini-war of succession. Parker's family and their allies claimed the ketchup for themselves, and the rest of the community said it rightfully belonged to society in general and, especially, to the unborn.

It was after Parker's family and their allies were defeated in war that Buddhism became the official religion of the post-Plague world. Supporters of ancestral ketchup inheritance were shown the error of their opinion when it was pointed out that Parker's reincarnated soul as a new baby would benefit from his ketchup being put back into the communal pot. The people were joyous, but not everybody was willing to chant and meditate. The leaders went easy on them.

The ketchup we were born with is the only certainty in this world. It's what we fall back upon in times of uncertainty or scarcity. It's what we use to trade for other goods that we've run out of like wooden boards or calendars or red pencils or cigarettes. Now, in a way, we are all born with Parker's ketchup and our world is wonderful.

PIT

"Raspberry jam makes me horny like a dog in heat!"

Hal screamed this right in the middle of the pit. There were ten people close enough for him to reach out and touch, and forty, fifty more jamming the floor. But Hal could have been yelling into the void of space; nobody heard. Tricky Woo was just too loud.

"The only time I ever did anything right in my life was when I tried a soufflé recipe out of Readers' Digest!"

It stank in the pit. Burnt hair and mustard. Farts and the insides of shoes. Salami and licorice. Hal bounced off a pair of unseen hands behind him and smashed into the back of girl in a sweaty red tank top and buzz cut brown hair. The back of her neck smelled like toothpaste.

"I often gorge myself with chewy granola bars and English muffins just before eating a big dinner!"

Buzz Cut flashed Hal a strange look as she pogoed next to him. "What?" she screamed.

Hal jumped in the air and crashed his shoulder against Buzz Cut's. "I said I often stuff myself with granola bars and English muffins before dinner!"

"What?"

Hal smiled to himself, secure in his anonymity. The floor was hard beneath his feet, hard beneath the stomping, jumping, moshing feet of everyone in the pit. Tricky Woo bounced about on stage, elevated four feet above the floor, illuminated in blue, white, and red. After crashing hips with Buzz Cut, Hal looked up and around at the horseshoe-shaped balcony, just under the ceiling of the club. He could see people in their seats, smoking and drinking and nodding their heads to the beat. Others had their arms stuck through spaces in the railing, slapping the balcony wall like hockey players slapping the boards in front of their bench to celebrate a goal or a good fight. Somebody, a brute, pushed Hal hard in the back, but Buzz Cut broke his fall, grabbing him under his left armpit and hoisting him back to his feet.

A tall guy with curly blond hair and a white undershirt jumped in between Hal and Buzz Cut, pumping his fist in the band's direction like a heavy metal madman. Hal hopped away, zigzagging toward the front of the pit where eight kids lined the stage. They kept themselves from being crushed against it by holding on to the stage with their hands and thrusting their backs and butts against the mass of slamming bodies behind them. Right behind the stage kids were the craziest thrashers: shirtless, zitty backs, protruding vertebrae, long hair slick with beer and sweat, bald heads beady with beer and sweat. These ones thrashed the hardest, flailing their arms, spinning their bodies like feeding crocodiles, smashing each other, once in a while hoisted up to surf the crowd. Hal moved carefully around the crazy ones. He slipped in between them and the kids lining the stage. He sidestepped to the far end of the stage on the right side, near the tall, brown, folded curtain. He staked out a spot in front of one of the big speakers and Tricky Woo blasted into his ears, so loud he could feel it dancing on his skin. He started in on the big confessions.

"I only own four pairs of underwear, so I wind up wearing the same pair on Thursdays and Fridays!

"I'm sexually attracted to the young Paul Newman but I'm sure I'm not gay!

"I hate Radiohead!

"I'm twenty-nine years old and I've only had sex with two women – one of them once, the other twice. I've only made out with six different women in my whole life, if you count the ones I slept with!"

Buzz Cut was coming back, pushing and bouncing through the crowd toward Hal. He wondered if she was doing it on purpose. She had a silver ring in the middle of her bottom lip that he hadn't noticed before. He liked the way her eyes were big and brown. She had tiny nostrils. She didn't have any zits on her face.

"Hey!" she screamed in Hal's ear.

"Hey!" Hal screamed back, yelling next to her ear but pointing his mouth down, just in case he spat.

"What are you screaming about?"

"I was just saying that I'm twenty-nine years old and I've only had sex with two women in my whole life!"

"What?"

Hal smiled. "I was just saying that I'd really like to know what it feels like to get blown by a girl with a ring on her lip!"

"I can't hear you!"

"I know! Isn't it great?"

"Great?"

"Yeah! Isn't it great?"

"Yeah," Buzz Cut screamed, nodding her head toward the stage, the band. "Great!"

The guitarist fell to his knees at the edge of the stage, right in front of Hal and Buzz Cut, sweat dripping from his brow, cheeks, and chin. He leaned back and shook his head like a lunatic, fingers twisting and twirling across the guitar strings. It reminded Hal of the way he played air guitar in his apartment. The stage kids ran over and crowded the area, reaching out to touch the guitarist. Buzz Cut pretended to go nuts and screamed like an old fashioned Beatlemaniac. She grabbed the guitarist's knees with both her hands. Hal spun and gyrated out of the miniature throng, leaving Buzz Cut behind, and stepped carefully between the edge of the crowd and the wall, fingering the change in his pocket as he walked to the bar near the back of the club.

It took a few minutes to get the bartender's attention, but Hal eventually ordered a draft. He pulled out a cigarette while he waited. He fished a book of matches out of a pint glass filled with them. The music was still blaring, almost as loud at the bar as in the pit. He tried to think of some new confessions for later.

"Can I steal one of those off you?" asked a voice from behind.

It was Buzz Cut. The ring in her bottom lip seemed to shine right in Hal's eyes. Her red tank top was tight around her skinny frame, her breasts pushing out round against the fabric. A thick wooden cross hung from her neck on what looked like a homemade chain of thin string. Her belly button was exposed, another silver ring inside it, surrounded by paper-white skin. Hal's eyes passed down to Buzz Cut's hips, snug inside black leather pants. She wore them tucked into her big green Doc Martens.

"I said, can I steal one of those off you?" Buzz Cut pointed with her chin at the cigarette pack in Hal's hand. "Fuck it's loud in here!"

Hal fumbled with his pack, but after a moment managed to open it. He extended his arm toward Buzz Cut, holding the pack open. She wrapped one hand around Hal's wrist, steadying it, and reached for a cigarette with her other hand. Hal felt a wave of warmth explode in the back of his neck, then pass through his torso. Her fingers around his wrist were pleasingly cold. Hal felt sick.

With the cigarette dangling from her lip, Buzz Cut brushed past Hal and reached into the pint glass at the bar, scooped out a handful of matches. She stuffed them into both her front pockets. "Got a light?" she asked, laughing at her own joke.

Hal lit his cigarette, pulled smoke into his lungs, reached out with the burning match. Buzz Cut took hold of his wrist again, and leaned her head forward, the cigarette dancing on her lips. The end of her cigarette ignited red, and she blew the match out with a puff of smoke. She let go of his wrist, but Hal could still feel the beautiful coldness lingering on his skin.

"I'm just here for the Woo," Buzz Cut said, blowing more smoke. "They fucking kill. Are you staying for Nomeansno?"

Hal wanted to reply quickly and smartly, but his mind took a while to process the idea that Nomeansno was probably the headliner. He never knew who was playing the Cabaret; he just came every Friday night.

"Can you hear me?" Buzz Cut asked, motioning with her head toward the stage. She stepped forward and spoke directly in Hal's ear. "Are you here for Nomeansno or just for the Woo?" Her breath touched Hal's earlobe gently as she spoke.

"I like Tricky Woo," Hal replied, speaking the first, only, words that came to mind.

"Yeah, I like them, too," Buzz Cut said into his ear, "I go to all their shows. Did you see their photo on the cover of the *Mirror* with all the private school girls in their little skirts? That was cool."

Hal nodded, figuring it was the appropriate thing to do.

"What's your name?"

"Um. Hal."

Buzz Cut nodded. Uncomfortable silence beneath Tricky Woo's noise. "Well, I'm Lisa."

Hal got with the program. "Hi Lisa."

"Hi Hal." Their arms touched, skin on skin, but Lisa didn't pull away.

"Hey you!" came a voice from behind the bar. Hal's draft was ready. He paid and tipped. He faced Lisa again with the plastic cup in his hand. She didn't look like a Lisa. He felt suddenly inspired. "You don't look like a Lisa," he said. And took a big swig.

"Thanks."

They smoked, looking at each other, then at the floor, the crowd, the stage, the bar, and then at each other again. Puff puff. Hal drank more beer.

"I gotta go to the bathroom," Lisa said. She took a last haul from her cigarette and crushed the butt under her boot. A column of white smoke funnelled out of her mouth, accentuated against the dark club background. "Walk with me?"

Hal coughed on smoke. "Okay." He offered the rest of his draft to Lisa and she downed it in seconds.

"So. You like to yell in the pit?" Lisa asked halfway down the stairs to the bathrooms.

"What?" Hal pretended.

"You yell and scream while the music's on. What are you saying?"

The answer came quicker than he thought it would. "I'm saying the words."

"Oh," Lisa sang, as if she didn't believe him. "What's your favourite song?"

"Um. The first one."

Lisa laughed. They reached the bottom of the staircase. Lisa headed straight for the men's room, and leaned her back against the door. She looked Hal in the eye and asked, "Would you be terribly disappointed if I told you I take my ring out before giving head?"

Hal didn't answer. He got a stomach cramp. Lisa turned and pushed on the men's room door. She put one foot inside. She looked in. And around. She pushed the door all the way open. "Come on," she said, fingering the ring on her lip.

Hal felt sweaty, especially in his armpits. His heart beat in his throat. His stomach cramp crept and crawled down his colon. Bye-bye Lisa, he thought. He spun and walked quickly away.

He farted as soon as he got outside the Cabaret, and his stomach ache was gone. He walked to Lafleur's. He ordered two steamies, a poutine and a Coke. In the booth, secure in his anonymity, Hal covered his late night snack in salt and confessed to his plate: "I'm scared of girls that like me. I'm so afraid."

WORKER'S COMPENSATION

My sausages are nearly ready.

They're a shiny shade of brown now, I'll just turn them in the pan a few more times with my plastic spatula. I move slowly, carefully. I listen to the pork juice sizzle as I jostle the links around. They hiss like snakes. I place the spatula on the stovetop, breathe for a moment, wait, then turn the burner down to zero. The sausages keep sputtering. Like me, they're in no rush.

I shuffle to the cupboard by the window to get a plate (a small one, I'm only eating four sausages), and I see that old beige sedan parked out across the street again. A little gleam of white light dances in the driver's side window. Keep watching if you want, I think, but you're not going to get much of a show.

I gingerly slide my sausages from the pan onto my plate. One falls, bouncing off my bare foot (Hot! But only for a second.) The sausage rolls across the kitchen floor, collecting lint and crumbs, and comes to a stop against the base of the wall. There's brown grease on my white skin and on the white linoleum. Which is whiter? I manage to make it to the kitchen table without dropping any more sausages, carefully cradling the plate with both hands, and set it down on one of my plastic Expo '67 place mats. I slide the chair out and get myself into it, no rush, leaving the sausage on the floor for the dog. She's asleep in the living room now, but she'll surely get to it before I have time to bend over and pick it up. I hope she'll lick my foot, too. It will be easier that way.

I take one of the sausage links between my thumb and forefinger and bring it to my mouth. I take a small bite. It's hot so I chew with my mouth open. I hope the lady in the sedan can't see that; she'll think I'm a pig. In my mind I tell her that I'm only chewing with my mouth open because the sausages are still hot. Once they cool down, I will eat properly. You'll see, properly and polite.

I take a second bite, put the sausage back on the plate, and wipe the ends of my fingers on my robe, riddled with stains that feel like wax. I'm wiping stains on top of stains. I would like to wash my robe but Kathryn only has "so much time" to spend on me when she comes over. Kathryn is always in a rush.

I suppose Kathryn learned how to rush around from our mother. Mom was always busy, always in a state of "going somewhere." My mother was never entirely at home. Even when her body was in the house her mind was on her next destination—"I don't have time for this, I have to get to work," "Quiet down, I have to get some sleep if I'm going to be in any shape for work in the morning," "Not now, honey, Seth'll be here any minute and you know he doesn't like to wait in the driveway." With so little time to spare, Mom never had the chance to read the cooking instructions on sausage packages. She never knew that frozen links are supposed to be allowed to thaw for five minutes in about an inch of boiling water before cooking them through. As a result, throughout our younger years Kathryn and I were treated to crispy sausages with burnt outsides and shockingly cold fillings. We ate them, though. Mom, our chef, didn't have time to take complaints from her customers.

My sausages are perfect. I follow the box instructions. I always get nice, soft sausages that are just as hot on the inside, if not hotter, as they are on the outside. I love my sausages. I wish Kathryn would try one of them some time, but she said she stopped eating sausages as soon as she learned to cook for herself and isn't about to start again now. I don't think she knows what a sausage is really supposed to taste like.

I learned how to cook sausages properly when I stopped working. Before that the only sausages I got were the ones in the Sausage McMuffins I used to eat before work. They were the only sausages I ever had time for. Sometimes, when she comes around early in the morning, I see the lady in the sedan eating Egg McMuffins and sipping coffee from a styrofoam cup. On garbage day, she even throws out her McDonald's trash in my garbage can. That is, on the garbage days that Kathryn has enough time to bring the can out to the curb. I like my garbage to go out regularly but I don't like to push my big sister on the issue, she's very busy.

I finish off my plate of sausages and wipe my hands on my robe one last time. I'd use a fork and knife if there were any clean ones. Maybe Kathryn will have time for the utensils on Thursday. I hope the lady in the sedan doesn't have any pictures of me eating with my hands. Or worse, video. I don't want her to think that I am a pig. Rather, I'd like her to know, I'm kind of sophisticated when it comes to the kitchen. I have the sausage box instructions memorized, I only have to quickly review the Kraft Dinner instructions before I whip up a batch, and I'm confident I could follow just about any cooking instructions out there if I had to. I've got time for that sort of thing.

I use the kitchen table to push myself up from the chair. Once I'm standing I put my hands on my hips and breathe for a while. Then I take the sausage plate in both hands and shuffle over to the sink. *Smile for the camera.* I would rinse the plate, make things a little easier for Kathryn, but I don't want to do too much. I don't want to make too much of a ruckus with the sedan lady out there. It's bad enough I let her see me cooking for myself but I was too hungry to wait. Kathryn has promised to buy some curtains for the kitchen when they go on sale somewhere.

I stack the plate on top of the others in the sink, on top of velvety globs of drying sausage grease from yesterday and from the day before that. I hope Kathryn will do my dishes soon. I look out the window and see that tiny, shimmering light in front seat of the sedan. I told Kathryn's husband Donny about it a while back and he told me to try and look as hurt as possible whenever I'm near the windows. I frown, not mad-like, but more sad. I try to make my eyes look blank, as if my life isn't even worth living. I hunch my shoulders. *Frown for the camera.*

I slide step down the hall to the living room. Kathryn and Donny pushed my bed in there last month so I could watch TV while I lie down and do my resting. The week after, the set blew and I'm on my third reading of February's issue of *Wrestling Insider* now. Kathryn says Donny will be over any day now to fix the television, he's just so busy with work and all. Don't worry, I always say, I know what it's like to be busy, to work.

When I worked, the bed was in the bedroom and the TV was in the living room, separate. When I worked, breakfast was at McDonald's, lunch was at the Swiss Chalet or Tim Hortons, and dinner was in a cardboard box in the freezer. When I worked, everything had a place because I didn't have time to start looking around for things. Now everything is all over the place; the bed's in the living room, the couch is over at Kathryn and Donny's, and I haven't seen my coffeemaker in over a week.

I sit myself down on the bed and the dog comes over, sleepy looking, and starts licking my foot. A little bath for my toes, and I'll take it since washing day isn't until tomorrow. Thanks, Trixie. Good dog. Trixie trots down the hall, her nails clicking against the floor, scouting out the kitchen for food. She'll have a nice surprise on the floor; my foot was just an appetizer. An appetizer, but at least I was good for something today.

I shouldn't feel sorry for myself. This is, after all, what I've always wanted. I have every day off now. I'm on vacation permanently. I never have to go to work and, even better, never have to be in that "going somewhere" state of mind. I have to be careful, though, that's for sure. I'm afraid if the sedan lady sees any improvement, catches me bending or reaching or walking fast, she'll take my picture and they'll send me back to work. But all this sneaking around is getting to me. My muscles feel like they're made of jelly. Kathryn told me that Donny thinks the lady's always out there because I've missed so many physiotherapy sessions. Okay, I said, but why would I want to do physio when all that's going to do is make me fit for work again?

Trixie is clicking back up the hall again, maybe she'll join me up on the bed. She'll have to go out soon. Where is Kathryn? Trixie is understanding in her own way about my situation. She doesn't bark or scratch at the door anymore if it takes too long for somebody to come by and take her out. She has simply adopted the empty bedroom as her own private place and, with the windows open all the time in there, it's really not that bad.

I burp. I can smell pork. A shimmering sunbeam has breached the living room window, a tiny dust storm billowing inside it. I hear the slam of a car door. I push off the bed and shuffle over to the wall beside the window, flatten my back against it and listen. Footsteps. On heels. Getting louder, closer. I lean my head in toward the window and sneak a peek.

She's coming up the walk, straight for my front door. I've never seen the sedan lady this close before. She begins to climb the stairs to the porch. She has straight, dark black hair, impeccably parted down the middle, ends curling in toward her jawline. A pair of rectangular, thick-framed glasses accentuates her slender face. Her eyebrows are angled sharply, alluringly, as if she doesn't believe anything anybody says, ever. She's so beautiful I think I might puke.

I withdraw my head from the window, lean my back against the wall again, close my eyes and take a deep breath. The doorbell rings. I don't move. I know it's coming and, sure enough, after less than a minute it rings again. I try to imagine her outside my door, waiting, but I can't remember what she looks like and panic sets in with a quick, unexpected intake of breath and a shudder that electrifies my shoulders. I throw open the door and she's right there. A breeze curls up under my robe, cools my knees.

"I'm really sorry to disturb you." The sedan lady gently raises a styrofoam cup from chest to chin level and smiles hesitantly. "I feel really stupid but could I bother you for a bit of sugar?" Her right front top tooth overlaps her left, slightly. "Idiots forgot to put it in the bag. I hope you don't mind."

I stammer, thinking of the answer. What Donny would say to say. Then Trixie brushes past me, tail wagging, clicks onto the porch, sniffs the sedan lady for a second and goes on by, down the stairs, the walk, toward the street. I call her but she ignores me. "My dog," I say.

"Your dog. I'll get her." The sedan lady gently extends the cup of coffee toward me. I just stare at it, terrified, for an awkward few seconds. She bends at the knees and carefully deposits the cup on the porch next to my front door. She turns to go after Trixie. She puts her right hand on the railing and starts down the stairs. Trixie barks.

The sedan lady raises her head and looks at Trixie across the yard and misses her step and goes down fast in a heap. I can't see her anymore from the doorway, but I hear her. "No. No. No. No. No."

I amble to the edge of the porch. The sedan lady is half-lying, half-sitting on her side, propped up on one elbow. One of her feet is on the bottom step and the other is just below it on the path. The bottom foot looks pretty busted up, the ankle good and twisted. Trixie jogs back and licks one of the sedan lady's hands.

"Are you okay?"

"Not really."

"I can call. Somebody. An ambulance?"

"Hold off on that."

"Pardon?"

"I need to get back to my car."

"I don't mind you waiting there."

"No, I can't be here. I'm not allowed to be on your property. Or maybe you already know that. I can't be here when they come to get me."

"I'll help."

"You're in no condition."

"And you are?"

I grab the stair railing with my right hand and stick my left arm out straight beside me, for balance. I start down the stairs. I teeter slightly. The sedan lady looks terrified and drags herself a few steps from the base of the stairs. I regain my balance and go slower. Trixie is yipping and dancing, waiting for me at the bottom. "No time for play, girl." I take the last step gingerly and toddle over to the sedan lady, work my way around her until my back is to the street. I bend down with a huff and take hold of her under the armpits. My hands feel meaty around her smallish bones. I pull, groaning, and the sedan lady helps out by pushing at the ground with her good foot. She stands, hopping, and leans against my enormous frame. I bend forward a bit so she can get her arm around my neck. I place one arm around her lower back to support her. Together, we begin to inch toward the street, her car.

"Petra, by the way. I'm Petra."

I stop. Pant. "Matt," I manage to blurt.

"I know. Thanks Matt."

"We're not there yet." I wipe the sweat from my brow with the sleeve of my robe and start up again. The sedan lady, Petra, winces.

"Sorry."

"It's okay. Not your fault."

With Trixie following close behind, we shuffle, drag and creep to the sedan. Petra directs me to the sidewalk and I help her sit down on the edge of it as gently as possible. From her car I collect her phone, hand it to her. "What are you going to say?" I ask.

"What would you?"

"Not sure."

"What about tripping over the sidewalk?" she asks. "What do you think?"

"Would tripping over the sidewalk be work-related?"

"Anything that happens is work-related. I'm at work."

"But are you allowed to get out of your car?"

"I'm allowed to stretch my legs." Petra points back over her shoulder with her thumb, toward my house. "Now get back in there." She smiles, pushes her glasses up on the bridge of her nose. "I'll give you a head start."

"You sure you'll be okay?"

"I'll be fine." She touches her calf, her face grimaced. "But, Matt: I won't tell if you don't tell."

I place one hand on my heart and one in the air, pledge of allegiance-style. "I saw nothing. Not a thing."

Petra reaches out with her hand and gives mine a warm squeeze. She releases it and I turn, whistle for Trixie. I make my way back up the walk, up the stairs, my dog following me inside the house again.

I drag a chair over to the front window and sit down. I peer around the curtain. Sitting on the edge of the sidewalk, leaning back slightly on both hands, Petra looks relaxed. Like she's at the beach. I'll miss her. But I'm happy for her.

My stomach's rumbling. There are more sausages to eat in the freezer. Maybe Donny will come by today to fix the TV, as a surprise. It's two o'clock in the afternoon on Tuesday and I'm not at work. I don't think I could be any happier than this or feel more free.

CREAMED CORN FINALE

"All you have to do is put the corn in your mouth and then let it fall out," Kevin said, cigarette dancing on his lips.

"Spit it out?" Gerrit asked.

"No, no. Just let it fall out. Like drool. Like you don't even notice it's coming out." Kevin dropped his cigarette into one of the empty beer bottles on the coffee table. Hiss.

"It'll get all over me."

"That's the idea. Exactly."

Kevin picked up the video camera from the floor and played with the focus settings. Out the corner of his eye, he watched Gerrit get up from the couch and walk toward the kitchen. Kevin lit another cigarette. He heard beer bottles clinking in the fridge. Then a loud crash – a kitchen chair knocked over, he surmised. Gerrit was a clumsy lout, but he was the only guy Kevin knew with a full-grown beard.

The downstairs neighbour knocked on his ceiling – Kevin's floor – at the exact same time that Jordache called from the bedroom.

"Kevin?"

"Sorry," Gerrit said from the kitchen.

Kevin tucked his new cigarette into an empty bottle, wasted, and got up from the couch. He lifted the bill of his baseball cap slightly and wiped his damp brow with the back of his hand. He stomped past the kitchen, where Gerrit was inelegantly replacing the chair to its upright position, and tiptoed down the hall. He gently pushed the bedroom door open, letting in a thin shaft of rectangular light. It illuminated Jordache's feet at the end of the bed.

"Are you nearly finished?" his girlfriend asked in the darkness.

"Jo, you know this is for school," Kevin whispered. He leaned one shoulder against the doorframe, his head just inside the room. His feet were turned sideways, though, anxious to get back to the filming. "Just a little longer, okay?"

"Okay, but don't let him sleep here."

"Not a problem."

Kevin walked back to the living room. Gerrit was guzzling beer. He put the bottle down on the coffee table, belched, and wiped his beard in one flowing motion.

"You ready?" Kevin asked.

"I guess."

Kevin went over to the corner of the room, where he had placed a can of creamed corn on top of one of his stereo speakers. He took the opener out of his pocket and removed the can's lid. Gesturing with the can at Gerrit, he asked, "You want a bowl or something?"

"Aren't you going to cook it?"

"Gerrit – it's creamed corn. In a can. You don't have to cook it."

"I'm not putting anything in my mouth that isn't cooked."

Sighing, Kevin made for the kitchen. He slopped the corn into a bowl and shoved in into his old microwave. He turned the dial to one minute, and it began to buzz like a small motor.

"Kevin?" Jordache called from the bedroom.

He took a deep breath and wiped his brow again. Gerrit was in the kitchen doorway, and Kevin brushed past him.

"You mind if I have another beer?" Gerrit asked.

Without turning around, Kevin said, "They're there for you, man." He adjusted his cap, pulled it further down on his head, tighter.

"Kev?" Gerrit called.

Kevin stopped walking, kept his back to the kitchen. "Yes?"

"You think we could order a pizza?"

"We don't have time. We're almost finished. Eat something from the kitchen if you're hungry."

Kevin opened the bedroom door, again just a crack. Jordache was lying completely still on her back, covered up to her chin in blankets.

"Are you cooking something?"

"It'll just take a sec," Kevin whispered. "It's the corn."

"What corn?"

"The creamed corn."

"Way are you making creamed corn?" Jordache turned her head to the night table. "It's two in the morning. Why are you making corn?"

"For the film, Jo. It's part of the movie."

"Why?"

Kevin sighed quietly. "Because the final scene is where Gerrit lets creamed corn drip out of his mouth."

"Kevin – it'll get all over the floor." Jordache was becoming more and more awake.

"I'll put newspapers down. Don't worry about it."

"Why do you have to make a stupid movie? Why can't you make a nice movie?"

"It's not stupid, Jo."

"It sounds stupid. Creamed corn."

Kevin began to close the door, his patience wearing thin.

"Wait!"

Kevin opened the door again. "What?" he said, tersely.

"I love you."

"I love you, too," Kevin said, pulling the door closed again.

"Wait!"

"Yes?" Kevin said, trying to sound nice.

"Kiss me goodnight."

"I already did! Four times!"

"Kiss me goodnight again."

Kevin sat on the edge of the bed. Jordache pulled her arms out from under the blankets and held them out to him. Kevin leaned in and kissed his girlfriend on the lips. "Now go to sleep," he said.

Back in the kitchen he found Gerrit staring intently at the microwave with a beer bottle in one hand. "Are you sure this thing works?" he asked, scratching his beard. "It's so old."

"It works," Kevin said impatiently; he didn't volunteer that he and Jordache only used it to thaw frozen meat.

"Aren't you afraid it's toxic or something?"

"Toxic?"

"It's so old. I could get sick."

Kevin let out a scoffing breath and waved Gerrit aside. He popped the microwave open. It was empty. He instinctively looked in the sink. The bowl was there, soaking in water, driblets of corn floating on the surface. "What happened to the corn? What the hell did you do?"

"You said eat something from the kitchen. It was ready."

Kevin wiped his brow. He winced at a little jolt of centralized pain near the edge of his right eyebrow; a new zit forming. "Gerrit, that was for the film. Remember?" He opened his food pantry and rifled through the shelves. He pulled out another can of creamed corn. "You're lucky I have another one. You're lucky I don't make you eat cat food."

"You're lucky I agreed to be in your movie." Gerrit placed his bottle on the counter. "Got any more beer?"

"My god, how many have you had?"

"A few." Gerrit helped himself to the fridge.

Kevin dumped the new corn into a pot and put it on the stove to warm up, scared that Gerrit's new-found fear of toxicity might render the last of the corn useless. He went to look for his pack of cigarettes in the living room, leaving Gerrit with the fridge.

"You mind if I—"

"Have whatever the hell you want – but not the corn!"

Another cigarette hooked in the corner of his mouth, Kevin set the camera up on its tripod. All the equipment had to be returned to the university by tomorrow. He could always renew it, he told himself, but the movie was due in less than a week and he only managed to reserve three hours in the editing room. Jordache was mad at him for putting so much work into the project and reminded him constantly that Intro to Film was only an elective class. He was neglecting his girlfriend and his marketing courses. But making the movie was so electrifying. Consumer focus groups and advertising theory didn't make his earlobes hot or make his head buzz. Even Jordache hardly did that for him lately. Film was the thing, but he still hadn't figured out how to tell his girlfriend he wanted to switch majors.

Another crash in the kitchen. Shattering glass this time. "Sorry," Gerrit called out. The downstairs neighbour banged beneath the floor. Kevin started walking toward the bedroom even before Jordache called him.

"What's going on now?" she asked in the dark.

"I don't know – you called and I came – I didn't have time to check," he answered passive-aggressively.

"Don't exaggerate, Kevin. Are you finished yet?"

"Not yet."

"Awww." She sounded like a crow to Kevin. He wanted to tell her to stop whining. He walked in and brushed her hair with his palm instead. "I like that," she said, sounding placated. Kevin made a sound with his throat to signify he'd heard her.

Gerrit was pouring red wine in the kitchen. "I hope you don't mind," he said, toasting Kevin with his wineglass filled precariously to the rim. "There's no beer left."

Kevin could tell that Gerrit had tried to clean up his accident, the broom was leaning against the counter, but little shards of glass still shimmered on the green linoleum. He wondered how long it would take Jordache to notice the missing wineglass. There was a long streak of red wine stain on the white window shade behind Gerrit. Kevin wondered how he had possibly managed that. The film, he told himself, on with the film. He checked the pot of corn on the stove.

"What happened to it? Where is it?" Kevin waved the pot in the air, empty save for creamed corn residue rimmed around the bottom.

Gerrit finished off the wine in his glass and licked a finger. "I threw it out. The can was damaged – the corn might be toxic."

Kevin glared at the empty creamed corn can on the counter. It did indeed have a dent on its side. He remembered paying twenty cents less than usual for it. "That's not true. It's just a dented can – Christ, never mind. That was the last of it."

He opened the cupboard to look for a replacement. There was a can of beets his mother had sent over in a care package three years ago. There were canned carrots, string beans, and mushrooms. Nothing looked right, though. He had envisioned he creamed corn for so long. It would have been an incredible finale.

He grabbed a can of black olives. Gerrit was refilling his wineglass with one hand and wiping his beard with the other, teetering slightly. Kevin put the olives back on the shelf; they would blend in too much with the beard. He took the beets down instead and reached for another pot above the stove.

"What are you going to do with that?" Gerrit asked, burping.

"Make you some beets. We're going to use beets."

"What do you need the pot for?"

"To make the beets." Kevin was losing patience.

"You don't have to cook beets," Gerrit said mockingly.

Kevin resisted yelling at his friend. He turned the can opener violently and dropped the beets into a bowl. "Let's go," he said, making for the living room. Gerrit followed with his glass and bottle in tow.

"Stand over there," Kevin ordered, pointing to the living room window. The camera, on its tripod, was directed at the spot.

"What do I do?" Gerrit asked.

"Put the wine down first of all." Kevin watched Gerrit finish off his glass, then carefully place it and the bottle on the coffee table, overcompensating for his inebriation. He stumbled back to his spot. "Now take this." Kevin handed him the bowl of beets.

"Kevin?" Jordache called out from the bedroom.

What now? he asked himself. "Wait one minute," he said to Gerrit. "Don't move. Don't move one inch." He left his friend standing, flimsily, the bowl of beets cradled before his bloated belly. "I'll be right back."

He went right in the bedroom and sat on the bed, hoping this would speed things up. "What is it Jo?"

She was silent for a moment. Then she sniffed and sat up in bed. "I'm thinking bad thoughts." She broke out into a stifled sob.

"Jo," Kevin sang, "everything's alright." But he was thinking: Christ not again. "What were you thinking about?"

"I don't want to say it out loud," Jordache whispered, her soft voice cracking.

"You should be sleeping."

"I can't sleep without you beside me. Are you finished yet?"

"I probably would have been finished by now if you hadn't called me," Kevin spat before he could stop himself.

"Fine. Go make your stupid movie."

Kevin took this as an out and left the room, shutting Jordache and her crying behind the door.

The bowl of beets was on the floor, and Gerrit had a cigarette going. "Put that out and let's do it," Kevin snapped. Gerrit stumbled over to the coffee table, took aim at an empty beer bottle and tried to deposit his cigarette into it. He missed, and the cigarette broke in two, dropping ash and dry tobacco all over the table. He put one hand on the table to steady himself.

Kevin approached and slipped both pieces of the cigarette into the bottle. He took Gerrit by the arms and eased him back in front of the window. "Just a few more minutes, big guy. Easy does it." He made a mental note not to provide his actors with liquor in the future. He backed himself behind the camera and started rolling, knowing he'd just edit out the directions he was about to give.

"Okay, pick up the beets and put as much as you can in your mouth." Gerrit nodded his head in comprehension, but didn't move any other part of his body. Kevin left the camera and picked up the bowl himself, thrusting it into Gerrit's hands. It slipped right out. Down on all fours, Kevin could feel the vibrations of the downstairs neighbour banging against the floor as he hurriedly placed the slippery beets back in the bowl. Jordache started calling him but he ignored her. Next to his head, Gerrit's feet did a slow and drunken dance of staying upright.

Kevin stood up with the bowl in his hands. "Open up," he said with a beet between his thumb and middle finger. Gerrit complied. Kevin placed the beet on his tongue. He grabbed another and placed it on top of the first one. In quick succession he slipped two more in sideways. Gerrit's beard bristles tickled the sides of his fingers. "Got room for a couple more?" Gerrit nodded yes, faltering a bit. Kevin held him up. Jordache called his name again. "One second!" he yelled. He stuffed three more beets into Gerrit's mouth, whose cheeks bulged, as if he had the mumps. Kevin heard him gag, and he stood ready to catch anything that came out of his mouth, but Gerrit recovered. Kevin dashed behind the camera and turned his cap around backwards.

One eye closed and the other looking through the eyepiece, Kevin appraised Gerrit's blue and white likeness. He looked perfect. He already looked ill; he wouldn't have to be asked to act it. Kevin heard the bedroom door open and Jordache's bare feet shuffling on the hardwood floor. He was sweating and wanted a cigarette. Keeping his eye on the eyepiece, Kevin raised one arm in the air. "Okay, slowly now. Start letting them fall out of your mouth. Slowly."

He heard Jordache coming up behind him. Without moving his head from the camera, he waved his hand at her, at once telling her to keep quiet and to stay back. One beet flopped out of Gerrit's mouth, bounced off his chin, and out of the camera's viewing range. Kevin waved his hand at Gerrit, telling him silently to continue. All of the beets flew out of Gerrit's mouth at once, and he doubled over, belching quietly and repeatedly. Kevin lifted his head, considered shutting off the camera, but immediately bent down to the eyepiece again. He saw some potential.

He watched and filmed Gerrit feel behind himself with one hand, trying to steady himself against the windowsill. Kevin heard Jordache walk around him, and then he saw her through the eyepiece in grainy blue and white, in front of Gerrit but a little off to the side. Again Kevin almost stopped filming, but more potential presented itself. Jordache's hair was a mess and the end of her thin nightgown was caught in the cleft of her backside, a think vertical line of concave cotton.

She turned to Kevin, faced the camera. "He's really sick," she whined. Then Kevin saw her flinch, and he raised his head from the eyepiece.

Gerrit was standing up straight, as if at attention, as if a six-foot metal pole had been inserted through his spinal column. His eyes were wide and scared. Then they closed halfway, his eyebrows arched inwards on each other in resignation. He slumped, half-sitting, half-standing, against the windowsill. He blew his cheeks out, puffed and round, his lips sealed. His head nodded three times. His mouth opened wide, like a yawn. A steady stream of half-chewed creamed corn, yellow and thick, spewed from his mouth and splattered on the floor. Jordache danced around on her bare toes like a ballerina, vomit splashing around her feet. Then she bent over, hands on her knees, and threw up on Gerrit's shoes.

"Cut and print!" Kevin called out, exuberant, laughing.

Neither Jordache nor Gerrit paid attention to his joke. It didn't matter. That a half-conscious oaf with a vomit-caked beard now lay on his living room floor didn't matter; that his girlfriend was crying and stamping her feet to the tune of the banging downstairs neighbour didn't matter; that Jordache would probably never, ever forgive him didn't really matter either. These were mere distractions. Small prices to pay for the creation of high art.

Kevin had his finale.

HER PLASTIC DAISY
AND THE CANADIAN WATER
TO GROW IT

It smells like Emily today. I cannot find the words to describe this scent, but then again, I never try. I could go on and on about her face, her hair, the clothes she wore; but to capture, in words, what only my nose knows is not only impossibly difficult, it's sacrilege.

We used to meet on spring afternoons beneath an old maple tree near the gates of Emily's school. I looked forward each day to seeing her face, her long, dirty-blond hair, her large, brown eyes, and the cluster of tiny freckles orbiting her small nose. Her mouth was also small, with thin wet lips. She refused to wear braces; she rather liked the little gaps between her four top front teeth and said orthodontic surgery was for the vain and unconfident.

When Emily and I met under the maple tree, I always wore grey flannel pants, a white shirt, and a thin black tie with yellow stripes; my school uniform. Emily had a standard plaid skirt-navy stocking-white blouse uniform at her school, but she managed to find little ways to stand out. Sometimes it was green nail polish, sometimes it was big, hanging earrings with crosses or stars or moons. Once she went a whole month with her hair tied up in red and yellow Jamaican braids, and the headmaster had to send four letters home before Emily finally had them removed. In the spring of 1986, Emily had taken to wearing a floppy beige sun hat she rescued from her grand-mother's attic.

I will not attempt to describe the scent that I am detecting so faintly, lest I betray the one last thing that I still hold sacred in this life, but experiencing it makes me believe more and more what the scientists say about the connections between memory and the sense of smell.

Today Emily's scent is especially strong in the basement, where I am gathering my tomatoes for the day. I pick ten with my wrinkled hands. My elbows ache each time I pull one from the vines. Most of the tomatoes are still more green than red, but I've little choice if I don't want to go hungry. I fill two buckets with water from my tank to wash my tomatoes in. Melvin the cat comes down, mewing like he always does when he hears the water splashing against the plastic insides of the buckets. I shoo him away. I already fed him his feline hydration tablet this morning. Melvin only thinks he's thirsty.

I stand over one of the buckets, hold a tomato to my chest and drop it into the water. The splash is refreshing. I continue with the rest of the tomatoes, releasing them for soaking one at a time. With each drop and splash, the concrete floor of the basement gets wetter, and I wiggle my bare toes in the shallow puddles. Emily's scent grows stronger when I play. The water in the soaking bucket is growing very dark, really brown; nearly finished. My toes are practically dancing in the wetness, and all these memories come washing back.

Emily liked the Cure, had the names of all the band members scrib-bled on her school binder. I liked the Smiths, but Emily found Morrissey's lyrics too depressing. We both agreed, however, on the merits of Gary Cooper.

I used to get to the old maple tree first, so I'd throw my books down and sit in the grass to wait for Emily to come. Sometimes I'd lie down on my back and peer up through the branches and leaves, to the bright blue spring sky. I imagined the sky was a painter's canvass, and I went through all of the necessary steps to create the finished product. First a large brush to cover the entire canvass in blue, then a round brush to produce the illusion of green leaves, and a thin, straight brush to add in the branches. The final touches would be to place shadows in the appropriate places, but that was delicate work for delicate hands, and I never tried, even in my mind. In my mind, I left that part for Emily.

The soaking is done, but before I transfer my tomatoes to the rinsing bucket I place my hands in its cool, clean water. I swish them around, imagine my whole body is taking a bath or, even better, that I'm swimming. I cup my hands together and snap them up quickly, splash my face with water. Drops roll off my chin, down my neck, and tickle my chest beneath my shirt. I'd stick my whole head in the water if I didn't need it to rinse my tomatoes. I give my face another splash. I run my fingers through my damp hair and shake my head. The end of my nose feels itchy; there's a drip of water hanging there. I stick my tongue out, like I was sticking it out at somebody, and try to reach for it.

Emily used to stick her tongue out at people. Like her older brother, Randolph, who would come around looking for her when we'd dawdle under the maple tree too long. "Come on Emily," he'd snort, not even looking at me. Randolph wore casual clothes in the spring of 1986; short-sleeved plaid shirts buttoned halfway, baggy khaki pants, and brown topsiders with no socks; he was allowed to dress this way, at McGill. Only a couple years before, however, when he was a senior at my school, he wore the same boring uniform I did, like everybody else at our boy's school. Now he was a man, or so he thought, a college man. "All right Emily, let's go. Mom wants you home. Don't make me drag you away." Emily would stick her tongue out at Randolph. He'd grab her by the arm and haul her off the ground, as if being her older brother gave him the right to be rough. I never knew what to do in that situation. I hated Randolph, and I wanted to defend Emily, but I was shy to interfere in family business. I didn't think it was possible to hate anybody as much as I hated Randolph when we were kids, when he used to make me feel so helpless. Emily would laugh while Randolph pulled her away to his car, though – he'd have to work hard to actually get her upset. She'd look back and wink at me. In '86, while her brother yanked her by the arm through the school gates, Emily would use her free hand to tap the top of her floppy sun hat, pushing the brim down over her eyes. I'd sit in the grass with my arms wrapped around my knees and try to smile, but all the while grinding my teeth and boiling inside – infuriated with Randolph but even more so with myself for letting him take Emily away from me. My only solace was the knowledge that we'd meet under the maple tree again the next day.

I can't reach the end of my nose with my tongue; I wasn't born with the appropriate gene sequences to perform such a feat; I was born in the days before parents could choose their children's genetic makeup. I wonder how many opt for the "tongue-touch-nose" ability, and how much a feature like that might cost. I wipe my nose with my thumb and lick the wetness from it. I dip my soaked tomatoes in the rinsing bucket. One by one, I turn them over and around in the clean water, then place them in my wicker basket. My hip starts acting up again, so I stop for a moment and stand up straight with my arms in the air, like the doctor told me to do when the pain gets bad. Stupid doctor. I hate him. Too young to realize that raising my arms in the air makes my elbows hurt. I wonder if he knows that, though; I wonder if he just pretends to know less than he really does. Some say when you hate somebody it's only because you recognize something of yourself in that person, something you don't like about yourself. I do my breathing exercises with my arms in the air, elbows and hip aching, and try to hold on to Emily's scent.

Emily never pretended. If something was on her mind, she let it out no matter the consequences; she never held back information or pretended to know less than she did. Like the afternoon in April of '86 when she told me she loved me.

I was propped up with my back against the tree trunk. Emily lay on her back with her head resting on my thigh, her hat shading her eyes from the sun. We were discussing how great Gary Cooper was in *Meet John Doe*. Other girls from Emily's school passed by on the path that led to the gates, staring at us. I remember thinking, hoping, that those girls would think I was Emily's boyfriend. We were sitting the way a couple would.

Emily suddenly turned over on her belly, her knees bent, ankles crossed in the air. She dug one elbow into my thigh, the other into my knee, and rested her chin in her cupped hands. Raising her head slightly, she peered at me from under the brim of her hat. I reached out with one finger and gently flipped up the brim. "I love you, Cecil," she said simply, softly.

My chest burned, right in the centre, and I thought my earlobes might have been glowing red. I took a deep breath, inhaling Emily's scent hungrily, and felt a tingle in the back of my neck, warm and cold at the same time. How long I had waited for that moment, and how easily she had come out with it. I reached forward with my face, straining my neck, and cocked my head slightly as I closed my eyes, seeking out Emily's lips with passionate sonar.

In the darkness behind closed eyelids, I felt the end of my nose swatted by a soft hand, and I heard laughter, giggling. I opened my eyes. Emily was rolling in the grass. "Cecil, you dork! I love you, I don't *love* you!" I didn't understand the distinction. I didn't want a distinction to exist. "I'm sorry, Cecil, darling, if I gave you the wrong idea, but I was just lying here, listening to your voice, thinking about how much I love you. And I do. But not kissing love. It's ... different."

I drop my arms to my sides again, tired from the breathing exercises. I am very lucky, to have known a love like that. I smile, and laugh out loud, thinking of my younger self, that boy, who didn't want to understand the difference between love and *love*. He had other things on his mind than the connection of souls. That's what Emily used to call it, I remember. She said we were two old souls, old friends, connected throughout time, always had been and always would. Now that I'm an old man and not just an old soul, I find myself looking forward to the time when the soul inside this withered body is released, freed to join its old friend. "It's been a long time," I say out loud, just in case Emily can hear. I begin rinsing the rest of my tomatoes. I hope all the things Emily used to say about us are true.

Emily devoured every text she could find on the subject of reincarnation and past lives. I remember one afternoon after school in early May of '86, when she told me about all the people we had been and the places where we had lived. According to her research, Emily and I first met in the year 1314, on a battlefield in Scotland.

I, apparently, was a ten-year-old peasant boy from Dover, sold into the English army by my family for an indeterminable amount of turnips, and had taken part in King Edward II's siege of Stirling Castle at Bannockburn. Emily was a bowman under Robert Bruce's opposing force and, during the rout that lifted our siege, had shot me with an arrow that stuck in my shoulder. Emily told me that while the English army retreated, I lay bleeding in the field among the other casualties. When the Scots came out of the castle, a wicked and corrupt man who wore Emily's colours went about finishing off the wounded and dying, goring them with his sword as they begged for mercy. Supposedly, this butcher turned me over in the grass with his boot, lifted his sword, and was about to stab me through, when Emily the bowman stopped him. She flung an arrow that whistled past his ear and warned him to back off lest the next one pierce his neck. Emily told me her past life-self had seen that the soldier she'd hit in the shoulder was only a boy, and then recognized me down on the field. She said I was brought to live with the bowman's family, rescued from prison and servitude. I thought it was a nice story with a happy ending, but not very believable.

"Don't tell me," I said with more than a little scoff in my voice, "the guy who wanted to kill me was Randolph, right?"

"Exactly!" Emily exclaimed. Her exuberance surprised me. "You understand, Cecil! Of course it was Randolph. Randolph has always been with us. He wants to hurt you, but he learned his lesson way back then: as long as I'm around, you're safe."

I laughed this off, though it actually made me nervous. I was about to make a joke about reincarnation, to make my scepticism about the whole thing clear, when Emily's eyes turned quickly to the school gates. "Look at her," she said, pointing to the street beyond. "Just look at her. Jessica Graham. Look!"

I looked, watched Jessica Graham open the passenger door of a long American car stopped before the gates. I saw her throw her school bag inside, then get in herself. I asked Emily what was so interesting and exciting about the sight of Jessica Graham being picked up after school by her mother. "Think, Cecil. Think! Jessica lives five, maybe six, blocks from here. She could walk home in five minutes!" I said, yes, she could, but wasn't it nice of her mother to come and get her? "No," Emily said, coldly. "No, it isn't nice at all. It's people like that, people who don't care, that are filling the air with pollution." Pollution? I wondered. I knew, of course, what it was; but I had thought pollution was a problem in California, in the United States. I had no time to inquire further, however, as Emily sprang from the grass and ran through the gates, holding one hand on top of her hat to keep it from blowing off her head. She waved at the car, then went around to the driver's side. I couldn't see her face when she bent down to speak, but I saw her hand resting on the roof of the car. I suddenly hated pollution almost as strongly as I loved Emily. The car peeled out with a screech. Emily looked at me from down on the street and hunched her shoulders. She put her hand on top of her hat again and ran back to me. "Oh well," she said. "At least I tried."

I place the last rinsed tomato on top of the others in my wicker basket. I think I'll eat half of them for breakfast, skip lunch, and eat the other half for dinner. The image of Emily running remains. I see her running to me even now.

"I've stopped eating meat," Emily announced a few days after chewing out Jessica Graham's mother for superfluous driving. "I told my mother last night. I refused to eat her pork roast."

I was sitting in the grass, leaning against the tree, Emily beside me. I asked her what she would eat instead of meat. "Vegetables, dummy. I'm a vegetarian now. And beans, lots of them. They're full of protein. Not those baked beans you get for breakfast, though: real beans. Chick peas, kidney beans, lima beans, black beans, all that stuff." I told Emily that she'd wind up with a flatulence problem if she ate all those beans. I was afraid she might get mad, but she laughed at my joke. I asked her what had prompted her to make this decision. "Because when I see meat now, I see the animal. I can't ignore the fact that bacon was once a pig, alive, that veal was once a calf, alive, that those nuggets they serve in the cafeteria were once chickens, or parts of chickens at least. I know this all started back in 1933, when I was a butcher in St. Louis – you know, when you were my apprentice and we had all that trouble with rats – and until now, I'd forgotten. But I can't ignore the connection between animals and food anymore."

I suggested she consult her family physician about this, to get more information before making such a drastic change in her diet. "Drastic? What's so drastic? Everybody thinks it's drastic. My mother had a freak. She said I was being silly. My father even put his newspaper down to tell me to eat the pork. I just sat there, sat on my hands. Oh, Cecil! It was beautiful! But you know, the real reason everyone freaked out was because they don't want me to be different. Me not eating meat makes them feel guilty about eating it. Randolph snuck into my room while I was doing my homework after supper, and he tried to stuff leftover pork down my throat!" I said Randolph was an asshole and I'd like to wring his neck. Emily leaned over and hugged me around the waist, pressing her face against my chest. "My hero," she said, laughing. "You're a real Gary Cooper." I thought about what life might be like without meat.

I lift the basket of tomatoes, holding it closely to my chest for support, and walk to the stairs. My elbow is pulsating under the strain to keep the basket aloft. I begin to think about the meal I'll have once I'm upstairs, and then another meal comes to mind, a steak dinner in 2019; my first taste of meat in over thirty years. I try to shake the memory, try to think only of Emily's scent, waning, but still present, still playing sweet havoc with my senses, my mind. At the top of the stairs I feel the cat brush between my feet, dashing back down to the basement to clean up after my splashing. I put the basket down on the kitchen counter, then place both hands on the counter to catch my breath. That damned steak comes back to my mind again. "Are you doing this to me, Emily?" I ask out loud, in case she can hear.

I take a plate from my dusty cupboard and lay one tomato on it. I think about the person who served me the steak, and how, by doing this, he was pretending to know less than he really did. I remember how I hated him even more then than I did before. By pretending to know less, by serving me steak and compelling me to eat it, he demonstrated his complete control over me. And I, pretending to know less than I really did, went along with the whole thing. I take the tomato from the plate and hold it in my hand. Elbow be damned, I squeeze with all of my might until it explodes, squirting red juice and white seeds all over my shirt.

The spring of '86 was the first and only time in my life that I actually did not look forward to summer vacation. The school day gave structure to my rendezvous with Emily under the old maple tree; it could be seen as one of many daily tasks to attend to. But it was no task, it was pure pleasure. There was nothing I loved and looked forward to more than meeting Emily at her school, and I feared the end of the school year would also bring an end to the routine that brought us together every day.

A week before the start of final exams, I walked to Emily's school, my backpack heavy with the books I was supposed to study from that night, and settled down under the maple tree to wait. I pulled a blade of grass from the ground and rubbed it between my thumb and forefinger. I placed it between my lips, let it hang there, just to see what Emily would say when she saw that.

Girls came down the path that ran beside the tree, some alone, some in pairs, others in larger groups. Many wore their white blouses untucked from their skirts and their socks rolled down; it was a very warm day. They passed through the gates laughing, chatting, outwardly giddy for the approaching end of the school year. One girl walking alone, a girl I'd never seen before, never noticed, turned from the path and walked toward the maple, toward me. She was a big girl, her plaid skirt stretched tight around her thighs, and she held her hands clasped shyly in front of her as she walked. The heat of the day had dampened her brow, and moist strands of her black bangs clung to her forehead. Little beads of sweat gathered in the crevices beneath her eyes. She looked younger than the other girls, but she was just as tall or even taller than most of them. She stood before me, still holding her hands in front of her, and opened her puffy lips to speak. "Emily didn't come to school today." She then turned and walked away, her message delivered. I was too wrapped up in my own self-pity to call out thanks. I pulled the blade of grass out from between my lips and threw it on the ground, angry. Angry at Emily for wasting a day when there were so few left.

It's taking almost an entire roll of paper towels to clean the mess I've made with the squeezed tomato. If I could use just a little water, the job would be so much simpler. But here, upstairs, it's out of the question. I wipe and wipe with the dry paper towels, but do little more than remove the larger chunks of tomato. I can do nothing about the stain; my shirt will have to be thrown away. A red smear is left on my kitchen counter, and I try to convince myself I can get used to seeing it there. I reach for a steak knife in my utensil drawer and put another tomato on the plate, carve out the hard, white middle with two clean strokes and throw it away. Then I cut the tomato into thin, round slices. Pushing the slices to the side of the plate, I take another tomato and cut it into thick wedges. Some variety today. The steak knife works like an extension of my own hand, I'm so used to cutting tomatoes. It's impossible to ignore, however, the tactile connection between my knife and the one I used to cut that damned steak in '19.

It had smelled exquisite. Emily may have compelled me to give up meat, but recognizing how good a charbroiled steak smelled was not a matter of choice. Still, I hated myself for enjoying the scent. Randolph sat at the opposite end of the long dining room table from me, no longer wearing khakis and topsiders, but three-thousand-dollar Armani suits and five-hundred-dollar leather loafers; the spoils of spearheading our private consortium that bought out the Crown Corporation for Arctic Water Systems in 2010. His hair was gone, replaced by a flat wig, combed more perfectly than the hair of a cadaver in a funeral parlour. His eyes still had a flash to them, though, and the family resemblance was startling.

When his servant placed the dinner plate in front of me, I looked up at Randolph, wondering how he could possibly have forgotten how I felt about meat. He just smiled at me, shook his head whimsically, and said, "Looks pretty good, eh? Flown in direct from Calgary, my friend. Nothing better."

I placed my hands in my lap and tried to recall a recipe for broccoli salad Emily had scrawled on the back of my algebra notebook so many years before. Deciding to eat that once I got home, I pushed the steak platter away from me on the table and began to update Randolph on our progress in diffusing the James Bay labour troubles. "Cecil," Randolph pleaded, playing the gracious host, pretending to know less than he really did, "not one word until you try this!" He made a big show of thrusting a forkful of steak into his mouth and rolled his eyes in exaggerated ecstasy as he chewed. "Go ahead: enjoy for a moment. Must you speak of business all the time? Go ahead. Dig in." I looked at him with puzzled eyes. I began to speak, began to say to Randolph you know I can't eat this, when he interrupted. "Eat it." He said it simply, harshly. I felt I had no will of my own.

As I begin on a third tomato, making more wedges with my shaky old hand, I wish for the will to end it all, to escape, to let the knife be my will, and to surrender to it as I surrendered to Randolph in his dining room thirty years ago.

The day after Emily missed our daily engagement under the maple tree, I brooded my way through the school day. I felt betrayed, left out. Emily never missed school. What could have been better than going to school and meeting me afterwards? I considered heading straight home, bypassing our place in the grass altogether, to pay Emily back, to make her feel what I had felt the day before. But when the final bell rang, my body reacted instinctively to the sound as it did every day; my heart beat more rapidly, my head swooned, and I couldn't get Emily out of my mind. I could not stay away from her.

On my way to Emily's school, I passed a flower shop. A few steps later, I turned back and went inside the store. I looked at the prepared bouquets kept behind a sliding glass door, I looked at dried flower arrangements in wicker baskets, and I looked at long stem roses in a big clay pot. Near the cash register sat a small display of lapel pins. Perfect. I bought a plastic daisy with white petals and a yellow centre that Emily could pin to her sun hat; I knew she'd just go crazy for it.

With my gift burning a hole in my pocket, I jogged the rest of the way to Emily's school. When the gates became visible, I noticed that somebody was already sitting under the maple tree. Who dared? I wondered. The person's clothes were not the uniform of Emily's school. I could see blue jeans, and a red shirt, maybe a sweatshirt. When I got a bit closer, I smiled as I recognized the beige sun hat this person wore. I redoubled my pace, anxious to be with Emily again.

I take a fork from the drawer and begin eating my tomato breakfast right over the sink. I don't care to sit down because I don't care to endure the pain of standing back up again. Chewing, I begin to feel guilty again about all the water I always use preparing my tomatoes, but I'm a man of a different time, when fruits and vegetables were washed before eating them. There's a knock at the door.

Outside stand six men in grey shirts, navy blue pants, and navy blue baseball-style caps. Security agents. "Morning, sir," pipes the one standing at the front of the gathering. He flashes an official-looking document in front of my eyes. The text is too small for me to read but I instantly recognize the Arctic Watersystems logo printed in the upper right-hand corner. "We have a Removal Order here, sir. One side please."

I barely have time to move before the whole group comes barging in. I follow them to the kitchen, where they begin milling about in front of the sink. "What are you removing?" I ask.

"A faucet," the apparent security captain replies, pointing to my kitchen sink. "Possibly two. The bathroom?"

"Down the hall," I say, trying to sound dejected. "But how did you know?" I ask, pretending to know less than I do.

The captain motions three of his men down the hall. "We have ways," he tells me. "It takes a while sometimes but we catch up with them all, eventually."

Good, vague answer, I think. I'm supposed to be scared now, scared to commit other crimes against the Corporation, what with their shadowy methods of finding out. But I know exactly how they found out. A lonely old man will do lots of surprising things for a little company, even call in an anonymous tip on himself if need be.

They're ignoring me, concentrating on the kitchen faucet, so I get the conversation going again: "What difference does it make? Why can't I just keep them? Are you afraid water might somehow begin to flow from them? Magically?"

"Sorry," the security agent says without looking up from his work, "wasn't my decision."

Of course it wasn't you, I think, because it was I who suggested removing and destroying all faucets in the first place; my final act before retiring from Arctic Watersystems, Inc. I close my eyes for a moment and silently recite as best I can from my own memo: *The physical removal of all faucets is the first step in removing the memory of running water from the collective consciousness of society.*

I lean against the kitchen wall, fold my arms, and note how young these security agents are; too young to know who I am, too young to know of my connection to Randolph Webster, too young to realize the marvellous irony in their act, in removing *my* faucets. Inert faucets while down in the basement my secret tank's reserves will continue to be replenished covertly on an annual basis by "agents" of a different sort as long as I walk the Earth. These innocents have no reason to look for it, to suspect anything; most of them were probably infants, perhaps not even born, when the water was turned off for good in 2028.

The men are finished their removals, two more faucets to melt down. The captain wipes his sweaty brow with his forearm and fishes a small plastic vial from his shirt pocket, pries open the cap. He shakes two green pills into his palm and pops them into this mouth – hydration tablets; poor bugger was thirsty. I let him and the rest of them out the door and watch them drive away in their navy blue Arctic Watersystems minivan.

Emily stood under the maple tree, leaning against the trunk. She waved to me as I crossed the street. She looked so strange in her jeans and red sweatshirt; I'd hardly ever seen her in anything but her school uniform. I waved back, hurrying to the gates. A familiar car was parked in front of the gates, Randolph sitting behind the wheel. I was angry. I knew our meeting would be a short one.

The steak tasted just as good as it smelled. So tender, each mouthful seemed to melt on my tongue before I had time to chew it. While it was a good taste, it was still foreign to me, in '19. I hated Randolph for making me eat it, but hated myself even more for complying. I tried to wash from my mouth the wonderfully terrible taste of skillfully prepared meat with big swallows of red wine. Randolph called his servant for more, said we'd need lots of wine, to celebrate with. I asked what we were celebrating. "Your promotion, Cecil." I asked him what he could possibly be talking about, reminding him the only upward move left for me at Arctic Watersystems was to take

Randolph's own job. Randolph said I was beginning to get the picture.

I darted through the school gates, jogged up the path, then cut across the lawn. As I approached the maple tree, I opened my arms, and I was filled with joy to see Emily do the same, welcoming my embrace. I could see her eyes were swelled up from crying, dirty streaks of dried tears splashed across her cheeks. I ran to her, and Emily ran to me. In the moment before we finally came together, Emily's sun hat flew off her head and landed in the grass.

I leave the tomatoes on the kitchen counter; I'm not feeling very hungry anymore. Instead, I go to my hall closet, push aside all the packages of paper towels inside, and reach into the back for an old cardboard box. I brush the dust from its top, leaving a dark brown smear on my palm. I bring the box to my living room and place it on the couch. I sit down beside it.

I told Randolph I still didn't understand; that it was impossible to promote me unless he was leaving the company himself. He told me to have another bite of Calgary steak, and he'd tell me right after. I complied. "Cecil, my old friend," he said, pausing for a big swig of wine, "we are about to embark upon the greatest financial windfall in history. Two chief executive officers working in tandem will close the sweetest deal of all time. We are going to be very, very rich." I shook my head, bemused. I wanted to tell Randolph that he was already very, very rich. Instead, I asked him to spell out his plan for me.

Emily hugged me long and hard. She squeezed me tight, and I squeezed back. "Oh, Cecil, it's terrible. It's just terrible," she moaned.

I took a step back, holding Emily's shoulders at arm's length. Her face was puffy and red. I let go of her shoulders for a moment, walked over to where her hat had fallen, and came back to her with it in my hands. I raised the hat above her head, breathing in her aroma. Emily put her hands up, though, blocking me. "You keep it," she whispered, pushing the hat back towards me, "keep it until I get back." Get back? I asked. Get back from where? "I have to go to Maryland, Cecil. I have to fly out tonight. I have to see the doctors there."

Sitting on my couch, I flip open the top flap of the cardboard box. I remove the crumpled balls of newspaper within, and dig in until I touch the soft, smooth, and rounded cotton surface of Emily's sun hat. I pull it out of the box and place it delicately in my lap. I devour Emily's scent, inhaling deeply, and it's more intense, more real, closer, than anything I'd smelled earlier in the basement. Without taking my eyes off the hat, my vision of which is blurred by swelling tears, I reach back into the box with one hand and scan the cardboard bottom with my fingers.

"Let me be the first to congratulate you on your new position at Arctic Watersystems, Incorporated, Cecil. The members of the board are all behind you, one hundred percent, all the way." Randolph pushed himself out from his seat. He walked all the way to my end of the table, extended his hand, and shook mine vigorously. "Congratulations, Mr. Chief Executive Officer."

I asked Randolph why I hadn't known about this before, how the board could go ahead with such an important decision without my involvement, how the board could name me to a position I wasn't even soliciting. "Haste is the key word," he replied. "We have to move quickly if this is going to be done properly. We both have to move quickly. You see, Cecil, I've been made an offer I can't refuse. I'm leaving Arctic Watersystems. I'm headed for the States to join EcoProperties, to head EcoProperties." I congratulated Randolph on his new venture, but told him I did not desire the top position at Arctic Watersystems, that somebody else should take the job. "No, Cecil," Randolph said, "the job is yours. You're the only person for the job. There's no time. A press conference is scheduled for seven o'clock. Tonight. And, you lucky devil, you will give that press conference. You will announce your first act as President and CEO of Arctic Watersystems on national television. You'll be beamed into every home in Canada! You, Cecil, you!"

I asked Emily what the hell was going on. I told her she couldn't leave, that I'd be lost without her. "I have to go," she said plainly, sweetly. "You don't understand, Cecil. I'm sick. Very sick."

My fingers find a rounded piece of plastic in the bottom of the cardboard box. I pull the daisy pin out, and hold it close to Emily's sun hat in my lap. A tear splashes on the pin, sucking up some of the brown dust on its surface, and I wipe it away with my finger. I unclasp the pin in back of the plastic flower and attach it carefully to the front of the hat. "For you, Emily," I say out loud, in case she can hear.

The white camera lights burned my eyes in the plush lobby of the Marriot Chateau Champlain. I sat in a cushioned chair behind a long table. I poured myself a glass of water from a plastic pitcher placed there for me. After taking a sip to wet my lips, I brought my mouth to the microphone and did what I was told, pretending to know less than I really did. I announced the merging of Arctic

Watersystems with the US company, EcoProperties. I announced the move would mean a boon for the Canadian economy, would translate into more jobs for Canadians. I pretended not to know what it really meant and denied the truth when it was presented to me in the form of journalists' questions. That is the job, the function, of a fall guy. I left the press conference looking the part of Arctic Watersystems' new, wise leader. I left the conference pretending not to know that I'd just sold Canada's water to the United States. I left the conference hoping Randolph would maybe summon me for one more celebratory drink so I could look again into those brown eyes of his that looked so damned much like Emily's.

I didn't hear the rest of what Emily said, the exact details of her ailment and the treatments she'd be undergoing, on that spring day in '86 near the maple tree, our maple tree. I was preoccupied by the terrible churning in my stomach, the frigid sweats I felt all over my body. My eyes burned with fear. I refused to take her hat. I told her nobody could wear that hat except for her. A smile appeared on Emily's serious face, and she began to laugh and cry at the same time. "Oh, Cecil. I don't want you to wear it, I want you to keep it for me. And anyway, do you think Gary Cooper would be caught dead in a hat like this?" I couldn't laugh at her joke, but she did. She pushed the hat back at me, pressing it hard in my hands, as if trying to make a permanent impression on my body. Then her face grew terribly serious, and she flung her arms around my neck. I wanted to wrap my hands around her waist, but I couldn't let go of the hat. Emily stood on her toes and closed her eyes. She pressed her wet lips against mine and kissed me long and hard. I wished I could stop time in that moment, live forever with my lips locked with Emily's, experiencing her kiss eternally. Inevitably, Emily began to pull back, she had to leave, but our bottom lips lingered for a brief moment, stuck together the way I knew, in that moment, that our souls had always been fused. "Goodbye old friend," Emily said with a wink, unwrapping her arms from around my neck. She put one finger to my lips and whispered: "Until we meet again."

I'm standing on a chair in my basement, and Emily's scent is stronger, closer than ever. I can't describe what it's like, it's impossibly difficult to put into words, and only I can know. My toes touch the edge of my secret water tank. I've removed its top cover completely, and the water looks calm, inviting. Down on the floor, Melvin is hunched over a big bowl of tank water I've prepared for him, lapping voraciously. "Drink kitty," I say out loud, in case he can understand. "Drink and enjoy." I dip one toe into the tank, and the water is cool. I'm holding Emily's sun hat, the pin I never had the chance to give her fastened to it; her plastic daisy and the Canadian water to grow it before me. I know she's going to just go crazy for it.

ACKNOWLEDGMENTS

For encouragement and feedback, thank you Janet Black, Michel Bousquet, JR Carpenter, KerryAnn Cochrane, Peggy Killeen, Claude Lalumière, Julie Mahfood, Elise Moser, Doug Simms, Donna Toufexis, Gavin Twedily, Elizabeth Ulin, and Helen Wolkowicz. For his sound and imaginative editorial suggestions, thank you Christopher Doda. For brotherly counsel of a titular nature, thank you Mike Paterson. For tireless administration of the Totally Outlandish Book Launch advisory board, thank you Nic Paterson. And, as always, for love and laughter, thank you Lynn, Anika, and Cate.

Many of these stories have appeared in magazines, anthologies and other forms of media: "The Doorknob" was distributed electronically by Airborne Entertainment to mobile device subscribers; "The IGA Kissing Bandit" in *Lust for Life: Tales of Sex and Love*, co-edited by Claude Lalumière and Elise Moser (Véhicule Press); "Hot Dogs on Everything" in *Carte Blanche*; "All the Way to the Dump" in *Matrix*; "Bester McNallys Fowl Tale" in *Lost Pages*; "The Ketchup We Were Born With" in *Island Dreams: Montreal Writers of the Fantastic*, edited by Claude Lalumière (Véhicule Press); "Pit" in *Blood & Aphorisms*; "Creamed Corn Finale" in *Lichen Arts & Letters Preview*; "Her Plastic Daisy and the Canadian Water to Grow It" in *Exile, The Literary Quarterly*.

Mark Paterson's first book of stories can be ordered from the Publisher by going to:

Recycled
Supporting responsible use
of forest resources
www.fsc.org Cert no. SGS-COC-2624
© 1996 Forest Stewardship Council

Printed in August 2007
at Gauvin Press, Gatineau, Québec